Land of
Ice and Fire

by

MARGARET MAYO

Harlequin Books

TORONTO • LONDON • NEW YORK • AMSTERDAM • SYDNEY • WINNIPEG

Original hardcover edition published in 1976
by Mills & Boon Limited

ISBN 0-373-02051-1

Harlequin edition published March 1977

Printed in U.S.A.

CHAPTER ONE

ALEX experienced a thrill of anticipation as the familiar rugged spectacle of southern Iceland came into view. She had always loved this land of contrasts and was looking forward to working among the friendly Icelandic people.

She had been surprised as well as pleased when her application for post of courier with Björn Einarsson Travel had been accepted, and had felt little regret on leaving England. Gerard was the only person who had really mattered, but after their quarrel last week even he had said nothing further about her proposal to spend the summer in Iceland; and now, as the plane lost height over the Reykjanes Peninsula, Alex wriggled excitedly, Gerard and England already pushed to the back of her mind.

It took but a few minutes to get through Customs and into the concourse, where she looked round expectantly for Björn Einarsson. Björn with a silent 'j', she reminded herself, remembering her difficulties with pronunciation when she first began to learn Icelandic. As the crowd thinned it became apparent that he was not there. Disappointed but undeterred, Alex was debating whether or not to take a bus into Reykjavik and find the offices of the travel agency for herself, when a man waiting on the other side of the concourse walked across.

Ruggedly handsome, with jet black hair curling into the nape of his neck and into long sideburns below his ears, he held Alex's attention for the few seconds it took him to reach her. 'It looks as though we're both out of luck.' He spoke in good English with only a faint trace of Icelandic accent, and when Alex looked up into his eyes she immediately forgot everything else. Smoky grey and thickly fringed, they held a powerful magnetism which caused her heartbeats to quicken uncomfortably. She smiled shyly before averting her head. What was happening? Even Gerard had never had this effect on her, least of all a stranger.

'Perhaps I can be of assistance, Miss—er——?'

Once more her eyes were drawn to his. He smiled warmly, appreciatively, and Alex felt an unaccustomed glow. 'Constantine. Alex Constantine.'

It was as though a shutter had been drawn over his face. In one brief second his whole attitude changed. He frowned, the grey eyes hard and questioning. '*You* are Alexander Constantine?'

Alex nodded. 'Alexand*ra* to be exact, but everyone calls me Alex.' She smiled, trying hard to ignore this sudden change of manner. 'And you must be Mr Einarsson?'

He inclined his head gravely before lapsing into rapid Icelandic. 'I'm afraid there's been a mistake. I was expecting a man. There was nothing in your letter to tell me that you were—a female.' He said the word derisively.

'And there was nothing in your advertisement to

indicate that you were looking for a man,' retorted Alex in equally fluent Icelandic. One of the conditions of the job had been an ability to speak the language and she had no difficulty in following his flow of words. 'I can't really see that it makes any difference. As I said in my letter, I spent several years here with my grandfather, and as I can speak almost any other language you care to mention I don't see what your problem is.'

He shook his head impatiently. 'I have tours planned in the Obyggdir and up Vatna Jökull. What use would a woman be to me there, especially if we ran into difficulties?'

Only five feet two in her bare feet, Alex suddenly wished for a few more inches. This dark man towered a good foot above her head and she felt at a distinct disadvantage. Drawing herself up as tall as she could, green eyes flashing, she said, 'It may interest you to know that I've crossed the interior many times, and climbed glaciers. It's clear you've never heard of equality for women.'

'Oh, I've heard of it,' he rejoined. 'Let's say I don't approve. I'm from the old-fashioned school who believe a woman's place is in the home.'

Like my grandfather, groaned Alex inwardly— and Gerard! Taking this job had been a sort of rebellion against her former life. Her parents had died when she was a baby and she had been brought up under the severe discipline of her grandfather, Charles Constantine. Her meeting with Gerard when she was seventeen had in no way eased her burden, for he held the same rigid Victorian views as the

7

older man. The two of them had got on admirably together and Alex had allowed herself to drift along in this unsatisfactory manner until a few months ago, when her grandfather died.

Gerard had taken it for granted that she would marry him and was highly indignant when Alex announced that she had applied for a job in Iceland. It had resulted in a full-scale argument, with Gerard declaring that if she carried out her intentions he would have nothing more to do with her.

It was ironical to find herself confronted by another man who held the same outmoded ideals, but Alex was determined not to be browbeaten. For too long she had allowed herself to be dictated to and was now prepared to fight for her rights. She stuck out her chin. 'And I believe that a woman should be allowed to follow her natural inclinations. If she wants to work, so she should. At least until she's married and starts a family.'

Björn Einarsson's well marked brows rose a fraction. 'Even if I did agree, which I do not, I still think you're not suitable for the job.'

'May I ask why?' Alex struggled to keep her voice even. This man was annoying her with his condescending manner and she began to wonder whether she had imagined the warmth in his smile a few seconds earlier. There was certainly no sign of it now. His eyes held a calculated hardness, and he looked as though he were assessing her qualities as a horse breeder might a filly's.

'You only have to look at yourself to answer that. A strong wind would blow you away. I need someone with stamina and strength—I need a man.'

'Appearances can be deceptive.' Alex gave an engaging grin, calculated to disarm this hostile stranger. 'Why don't you give me a try? I'll soon prove that I'm tougher than I look.'

He shook his head, a brief flicker of his eyes the only indication that he was aware of the attractiveness of her smile. 'I can't afford the risk. This is my first season in business and I don't want to fail.' He consulted his watch. 'Unfortunately there are no more flights tonight. I'll take you to your hotel. You can catch the first plane back to London in the morning.'

Without giving Alex time to argue he picked up her cases and led the way to the parking lot. Stopping at a yellow Volkswagen, he stowed her bags into the boot and opened the passenger door. He made no further attempt to speak as they headed towards Reykjavik. Stealing a glance at his profile, Alex could see by the determined set of his chin that as far as he was concerned the matter was closed.

'Isn't there anything I can say to make you change your mind?' she persisted.

He didn't even look at her. 'Nothing. I'm sorry it's happened like this and naturally I'll pay your return fare, but there's nothing more to be said.'

'I think you're being unreasonable,' returned Alex. 'I wouldn't let you down. I know Iceland almost as well as you do.'

'I've no doubt,' came the even reply, 'but the answer's still no.'

'Men!' snorted Alex, more to herself than her

companion. Why did they always assume she was incapable of holding down a job? She was twenty-two now, and had never been allowed to work in an office or a shop as did other girls of her own age. Her place had been at home, acting as hostess to Charles Constantine's innumerable friends, or working on a piece of embroidery or tapestry to pass away the hours. Her own friends had envied her easy life, but Alex had felt frustrated, tied down by circumstances. She could have rebelled, left home even, but she had loved the old man dearly in spite of his ways and she would do nothing to hurt his feelings.

At this moment it seemed that even her newly-acquired freedom had not given her the release she desired; Björn Einarsson had turned out to be a carbon copy of her grandfather. She sighed deeply, depression dampening her exuberance of a few minutes earlier.

She felt rather than saw her companion glance quickly in her direction before concentrating once again on the road ahead.

'You don't appear to have a very good opinion of my sex,' he said quietly.

'Why should I?' Alex's eyes flashed. 'They don't seem to have a very high opinion of me, except to make sure that I'm protected from the evils of life.' She warmed to her subject. 'No one ever allows me to do anything that I want to do. I'm expected to sit and look pretty and make myself useful round the house.' She missed his brief smile. 'But I intend to alter that. Even if you won't give me a job, Herra

Einarsson, I shall find work somewhere. Not everyone thinks the way you do.'

'You're probably right, and I'm sorry I have to turn you away. It would be pleasant working alongside such an attractive young woman.'

Alex's eyebrows shot up. 'You say that—after the way you spoke earlier? If those are your inclinations why don't you follow them?'

'We can't always do what we want in this life,' he responded. 'My immediate plans do not include a female courier and no amount of persuasion on your part will make me change my mind.' He slanted her a smile, as if trying to take the sting out of his words. For an instant Alex saw again the friendly stranger, felt her own instinctive response, before the barriers were once more erected.

Realising it would be futile to argue further, she lapsed into silence for the remainder of the journey. The fifty kilometres to Reykjavik were soon covered and Björn Einarsson drove into the eastern sector, where he pulled up in front of the impressive glass-fronted Hotel Esja. Alex felt surprised that he should go to the expense of booking a room here at one of Reykjavik's largest and newest hotels—even though he had expected a man he would still have been Björn Einarsson's employee, so surely a more modest hotel would have been adequate? Perhaps he's trying to create an impression, thought Alex drily, though she couldn't imagine why.

Once she had signed the register and obtained her key he left, with the strict injunction to be ready at nine sharp in the morning. Despite the way he had treated her Alex felt a stab of disappointment at his sudden exit. It would have been nice to have company during the remaining hours of the evening, even someone as distant as Björn Einarsson.

She took the lift up to her room, not really appreciating the luxury of her surroundings. Her mind still dwelled on this puzzling man and why he was so set against a woman working for him. Perhaps he has a grudge against women in general, she surmised, perhaps he's been thwarted in love and has now turned against the fairer sex. But he hadn't been so cool to start with. It had only been when he discovered her identity that the real trouble began. No, it had to be the job—though his attitude didn't make sense, no matter how much she mused over it.

She bathed and changed and made her way to the grill room at the top of the building. It commanded magnificent views over the city and the surrounding countryside, and as Alex looked out an idea began to form in her mind.

Why shouldn't she remain here in Iceland? She had enough money to last until she found another job; her grandfather's friend, Jón Karlsson, would help there. In fact, it might be a good idea to ring him now. If she had everything arranged, Björn would be unable to insist that she return to England, for she knew he would. If her assessment of him was right he would certainly be against the idea of her remaining here alone.

Hurriedly Alex finished her meal and returned to her room. She found Jón Karlsson's number in her address book and soon she was through.

'Alex!' He sounded surprised. 'Where are you?'

'I'm here—in Reykjavik,' she told him. 'I'd like to see you. I need your help.'

'You're not in trouble?'

'No, no, nothing like that. I need a job.'

He laughed then. 'You must be joking. Don't say Charles left you penniless?'

'Hardly, but I'm bored doing nothing.'

'You must stay with Helga and me,' offered Jón, 'I'll come and pick you up. Why didn't you let us know?'

'I had a job—or so I thought—but it's fallen through and I don't particularly want to return to England just yet. I've a room booked for tonight at the Esja, but I'll come and see you tomorrow if I may?'

'There'll be trouble if you don't,' he threatened, 'Helga's making frantic signals here. I'll fetch you first thing in the morning.'

'Thanks a lot, Jón. I knew I could rely on you.'

Alex felt better after that, deriving a certain amount of pleasure at the thought of Björn Einarsson's face when she told him she was staying. She couldn't yet weigh him up. He was attractive—certainly the most interesting man she had ever met—the way her pulses raced when they first met proved this. Perhaps it was as well they were not working together, he could be a dangerous friend. He had probably not thought twice about her, apart from the fact that she possessed her fair share of good looks. The raven black hair which curled silkily around her face was one of Alex's best features and one which had caused many a man to take a second look, but this did not account for the way she had reacted, and there was nothing to indicate that this Icelander felt the same way about her—in fact, after the way he had behaved it seemed as though he were completely uninterested.

Throughout the entire evening Alex could not dismiss him from her thoughts. Although she knew that after tomorrow it was unlikely they would meet again, he had somehow inextricably woven himself into her mind. The deep-set smoky eyes and the full, warm smile haunted her. For ever she would remember him as he crossed the concourse, the confident, self-assured walk, the impeccably-cut overcoat, the air of breeding. Here was a man who could have swept her off her feet—if only he had held different views.

Perhaps it was fortunate the way things had turned out. She might have lived to regret ever meeting Björn Einarsson, for there would surely be clashes of temperament if they were thrown together for long periods.

Promptly at nine the next morning Björn arrived, and Alex was in reception waiting. He smiled when he saw her. 'Are you ready? If so, we'll go. I haven't much time.'

Alex returned his smile but spoke coolly, trying hard to ignore the sudden warmth created by his presence. 'I'm not coming. I've decided to stay in Iceland after all.'

His reaction was as she expected. Bushy brows

knit together, his eyes hardened and narrowed. 'What is this? Some kind of joke? If so, I'm not amused. Please fetch your coat and let's go.'

Alex countered his gaze. 'It's no joke. I'm staying. I came here intending to do a job of work, and if you won't employ me I'll find someone who will.'

'This is ridiculous.' He shook his head impatiently. 'You can't wander round a strange country on your own.'

Alex smiled. 'You forget I've spent many years here. And I have friends. Please don't worry on my account.' She held out her hand. 'It's been nice meeting you, Herra Einarsson. I'm sorry you've been disappointed.'

He ignored her hand. 'You're mistaken there, Fröken Constantine, I have no regrets, merely an anger that I stupidly did not check your identity before bringing you here.'

'That's my fault. Please don't feel annoyed with yourself.'

He lifted his brows. 'Do you suggest I take it out on you? I may have some peculiar ideas, but blaming a woman for something that is not her fault is not one of them.'

'Then I'm sorry you feel like this—and I apologise,' said Alex warmly.

He inclined his head. 'Now perhaps you'll tell me exactly what you propose doing? Having got you over here I feel responsible. I can't just leave you like this.'

It was nice of him to feel concerned, and Alex experienced a glow which she was sure must be reflected in her eyes. She turned away, loth to let this man see the effect he had on her.

'I have a friend calling for me shortly. I'm staying with him until I find a suitable job.' He had moved into her line of vision and the look on his face was enough to tell Alex that he had misinterpreted her statement. She toyed with the idea of allowing him to think the worst, then realised that she didn't want this. For some unknown reason it was important that he should receive only a good impression. 'And his wife, of course. They were very dear friends of my grandfather.'

She had not been mistaken. The relief on his face was evident. 'And may I ask the name of these good friends?'

'Certainly,' smiled Alex, 'but I shan't tell you. I don't want you checking on me. As far as I'm concerned there's nothing more to be said.'

'I'm sorry you feel like that,' he said stiffly, 'I thought that perhaps we could be friends.'

The grey eyes looked sad for a moment, causing Alex to frown suspiciously. 'I was under the impression that you were glad to get rid of me.'

He nodded slowly. 'As far as the job goes, yes, but socially I'd be only too pleased to see you.'

And me you, thought Alex breathlessly. But it wouldn't be wise. She had seen what a pedantic man he was, the type she wanted to avoid at all costs. This was a case where her head must rule her heart or she would find herself with another all-dominating male to contend with. 'You surprise me, but the answer's still no. I don't really think we have anything in common. Goodbye, Herra Einarsson. I really must go now.'

This time he took her hand. As he did so Alex became aware of a tingling sensation along her spine and a tightening at the base of her throat. She swallowed painfully and avoided his eyes; it was ludicrous that a comparative stranger should have this effect on her. She was crazy, and the sooner he went the better. No one else had ever disturbed her in this manner. Why did it have to be him? Why couldn't she have been attracted to a nice young man with the same modern outlook as herself?

'Goodbye—Alexandra.'

Alex's heart gave a quick jerk at the sound of her name. Everyone else called her Alex and she preferred this shortened version, but there was something in the way he had said Alexandra that sounded almost like an—endearment. It was silly, she knew, and probably it was only imagination, for there was nothing on his face to suggest he meant it this way.

'I hope everything turns out all right. If you do need help at any time, you know where to find me.'

Her fingers still lay in his and Alex had difficulty in meeting his gaze. 'Thank you, but I don't think that will be necessary.' Quickly she withdrew her hand and walked away. Any minute now he would notice her reaction and before she knew it she would find herself agreeing to meet him again. At this moment it was what she desired most in the world, but she must be strong—brush away these insane desires. The Björn Einarssons of this world were not for her.

Unable to resist a backward glance as she entered the lift, all Alex saw was the back of his head as he disappeared through the doors. Disappointment welled. She had somehow expected him to watch her go. It shows he has little real interest, she thought, but why should I care? He's not my type at all.

It was easy to tell herself this, but it was not so simple to dismiss him from her thoughts. She was glad when the telephone rang and she was told that Jón Karlsson waited downstairs. At least now she would have something to take her mind off that disturbing Icelander!

Jón Karlsson, a thin, grey-haired man, looking nothing like his sixty-eight years, walked briskly towards Alex as she emerged from the lift. He held out both hands and greeted her warmly.

'Alex, it's good to see you. I was awfully sorry to hear about your grandfather, and I must admit Helga and I wondered if we'd ever see you again. She was so excited after you'd phoned.'

'Not as pleased as I am to be back in my beloved Iceland,' Alex said. 'I should have come some time, Jón, believe me. In fact I wouldn't mind settling down here.'

Jón laughed. 'As full of enthusiasm as ever, I see! All you've got to do is find yourself a nice Icelander to fall in love with. If I were forty years younger and fancy free, I'd marry you myself.'

Alex joined in his laughter. 'I do love you, Jón. I feel better already.' She had always been fond of this friend of her grandfather. He was so different from Charles that it was difficult to imagine there had ever been a bond between them. Jón would never object to her working, of this she was sure. In fact he'd said on several occasions that if she ever wanted to live in Iceland he would be only too pleased to help.

'I'm sure things aren't that bad,' he said. 'Come, you can tell me all about it on the way.'

It was only a short distance from the Esja to Jón's home, but in that time Alex told him about the job—all she omitted was Björn's name, for she was afraid of giving away her feelings. The mere thought of him made her blood pump more urgently and she cursed herself for falling for such a man. She had heard that love could come with a bang—and this certainly had. For that was what it was, without a doubt. Why else would she feel so breathless and weak at the mere touch of his hand or the warmth of his smile? She closed her eyes. It was painful, this falling in love—heartbreaking too, when it was with the wrong man.

Helga and Jón lived in the old part of the town near the lake. In common with most of their neighbours the house was painted white, and had a bright green roof. The first time Alex had arrived in Reykjavik by air she had been enchanted by the medley of colourful roofs, blue and red, green and purple, looking for all the world like a toy town. The image was lost once in the city, but even so she never failed to appreciate its bright cleanliness.

The door opened immediately they pulled up outside the house and Jón's wife, smiling as always, came down the path to meet them. Helga Péturs-dóttir had reached old age gracefully, as tall and slim as her husband, and her skin had retained the firm freshness of youth. Her hair, though white as snow, framed her face in a cluster of curls. When asked to what she attributed her good health she would state firmly that the right foods and Iceland's unpolluted air were the answer.

When Alex had first visited Iceland she could never understand why a husband and wife should have different surnames until she found out that a woman did not change her name when she married. To further complicate matters, when a child was born his surname was composed of his father's christian name followed by *son* if he was a boy or *dóttir* if a girl. Therefore Jón was Jon Karlsson, son of Karl, and Helga was Helga Pétursdóttir, daughter of Pétur.

Alex had always looked on Helga as the mother she had never known, and as the older woman came towards them she jumped out of the car. Welcome arms clasped her and Helga's eyes were suspiciously bright as she greeted old Charles's granddaughter. 'You ought to have come to us yesterday,' she scolded lightly, 'instead of staying in that hotel all by yourself. You know you're more than welcome.'

'Of course I do, Helga dear! But as I've just explained to Jón, I came over for a job as courier. I didn't even know if I'd have time to come and see you.'

'There'd have been trouble if you didn't,' replied Helga.

Alex laughed. 'Oh, I'd have come, but I'm not sure when. Anyway, the job's fallen through, so—here I am.'

'You must tell me all about it, but first of all let's go inside. Have you had breakfast?' and as Alex nodded, 'I'll make coffee.'

Alex knew it would be futile to argue. Helga would be offended if she didn't have something. She was never happier than when working in her kitchen.

They left Jón to garage the car and bring in Alex's cases. The house was as bright and sparklingly clean as Alex remembered it, with the smell of lavender polish still in the air. In the kitchen, full of ultramodern devices, Alex perched on a stool while Helga tipped coffee beans into the grinder before filling the kettle.

'It's good to be back,' smiled Alex contentedly. 'I'd like to live in Iceland.'

'Well, what's to stop you?' inquired Helga. 'You've no ties back home now—or is it that young man of yours, Gerard Fisher?'

'Gerard!' Alex pulled a face. 'I hardly think so. He's not my type.'

'But I thought——' Helga frowned. 'I thought you and he were— Surely Charles said you were the best of friends?'

'It's what Grandfather would have liked,' admitted Alex, 'but since he died I've realised how much I've been tied down. If I married Gerard life would be no different. I've had enough, and I want to be free. Free to do what I like.'

Helga looked worried. 'I've never heard you talk like that before. I always thought you were perfectly happy.' ·

'Don't get me wrong, Helga, I wasn't unhappy. Grandfather was an angel. But I was tied down by circumstances. I could have rebelled, but I wouldn't, I loved him too much for that. But if Gerard thinks I'm going to spend the rest of my life meekly agreeing to his every wish, he's got another think coming. He didn't like me coming here, you know; we had a row. I wouldn't be surprised if I never saw him again.'

Helga looked at her wisely. 'And you don't mind?'

'Not at all,' shrugged Alex. 'Why should I? He never really meant anything to me. He was Grandfather's friend more than mine. I suppose he thought we would get married one day.' She laughed suddenly. 'I can just imagine him asking Grandfather's permission and then getting down on his knees to ask me. He's like that, very Victorian.'

'You're unkind,' said Helga, passing her coffee. 'I'm sure he was a very nice young man.'

'You never met him, or you'd see what I mean. 'Anyway'—Alex lifted her chin in a gesture of defiance—'I've put Gerard completely out of my mind. I'm going to find myself a job here and, who knows, I may end up staying in Iceland for ever. That's where I want your help. I'm sure you and Jón must know someone who needs a—well, someone who can find me a job.'

Helga smiled and nodded. 'I'm sure we can, though it won't be easy. It's not as though you've trained for anything.'

'That's Grandfather's fault, not mine,' sniffed Alex.

'What happened to this courier job? I would think that's just your line. You must know Iceland as well as you do England.'

Alex smiled. 'I was the wrong sex. He wanted a man, it's as simple as that.' And before Helga could question her further she continued, 'This is marvellous coffee. We always use the instant kind back home, but it tastes nothing like this.'

Helga was pleased. 'You can't beat freshly ground coffee. Would you like another cup before you unpack? I've put you in your usual room overlooking the lake.'

'Thanks, Helga. I wasn't looking forward to hotel life.' Relieved that the older woman had not questioned her further about the job, Alex lapsed into silence. As with Jón, she felt loth to discuss Björn Einarsson. She hated herself for being attracted to him; he was everything she sought to escape. Charles and Gerard—they both had the same ideas, the same views—thoroughly outdated views in Alex's opinion. She must forget Björn, and the only way to do so was never to speak, or even think of him again. Easier said than done, but if Helga and Jón didn't know about him there would be no chance of them bringing him into the conversation.

'You don't have to work,' said Helga, 'you can stay with us for as long as you like.'

They had no family and Alex knew that both Helga and her husband enjoyed company. 'Thanks for the offer,' she said, 'but I feel my life's being wasted. I can't go on like this. I want to do something useful, something satisfying.'

'I'm inclined to agree with you,' smiled Helga, 'there's nothing like a healthy day's work for keeping the body young and active. I can't bear to be idle myself, so I know how you feel.'

Pleased that her friend was in agreement, Alex smiled at her and then went to her room. It took no time at all to unpack and when she went down again Jón was using the telephone. Judging by his reaction he was not having much luck, and Alex began to realise how difficult it would be for her to get work. If only she had trained as something—a typist, a book-keeper, a nurse maybe—but she had done nothing. She had idled away her hours as best she could. She knew how to run a house, could cook, sew or embroider with considerable skill, but where did that get one in so far as a job was concerned? She didn't fancy a job as a housekeeper or nannie, it would be no better than the life from which she was escaping. No, the courier's job would have been ideal. It took no special skills, merely a knowledge of the country and an ability to organise people.

The day seemed long, and at last Jón confessed he could do nothing for her. 'I've asked everyone I know, but with no qualifications it's difficult. I'm sorry, Alex—but you will stay?' He seemed anxious.

'Of course,' smiled Alex. 'Anyway, I've not given up hope. Something will crop up, I know.' Had she foreseen the future, she might not have been so cheerful.

The following morning she went shopping with Helga. 'We have a visitor this evening,' explained the older woman as she carefully selected an assortment of lightly pickled meats, to be eaten with rye bread, brown wholemeal or white, according to taste. 'His father was a friend of Jón's. He's about your age, so you should get on well together.'

Alex was in her room changing when the visitor arrived. She could hear the murmur of voices and quickly put the finishing touches to her hair. One last glance in the mirror revealed an elf-like creature in deepest green, cheeks flushed through hurrying, almond-shaped eyes reflecting the colour of her dress and black hair swept upwards into a more sophisticated style for the evening. It gave her the extra height she needed and, humming softly to herself, she went downstairs.

The door to the dining-room stood ajar and Alex's breath caught in her throat as she heard the sound of that well-remembered voice.

'Imagine my disgust when she turned out to be a girl. I ask you—in a job like that!'

Alex's lips tightened. How dared he? What right had he to discuss her like this? Did Helga and Jón know it was Alex herself who was involved? Before stopping to think she burst into the room. He was not going to get away with this.

'Good evening, Herra Einarsson, I see you still find my application surprising. I wish I knew why.'

'You!' He stared at her for a full five seconds before looking questioningly at his host and hostess. 'Why didn't someone tell me?'

Helga shook her head, as though unable to comprehend what was happening.

'Maybe I should explain.' Alex crossed the room and slipped her arm through the older woman's. 'This is the man who refused me the job. I wish now I'd told you his name, it would have saved us both the embarrassment of meeting like this.'

By now Björn Einarsson had recovered from his surprise. 'I apologise, Fröken Constantine, if I've offended you. I think perhaps it would be best to let the matter drop. I have no wish to cause my good friends here any unpleasantness.'

'Unpleasantness!' echoed Alex. 'I like that! With all due respect to present company I think it's I who have suffered, and I should like to——'

She stopped as Helga pressed her arm in a silent pleading gesture, and smiled wryly. 'I'm sorry, Helga. I'll try and forget who he is—just for you and Jón. I don't want to spoil your evening.'

Surprisingly, Björn held out his hand. 'Let's call it a truce. I don't want my evening ruined either.'

Unable to help herself, Alex softened and placed her hand in his, closing her eyes at the involuntary racing of her pulses. She was bewildered by her own reactions. Hadn't she proved that there could never be anything between them? Then why did she react

26

like this? She felt confused and not a little disturbed.

He was watching her closely, a curious expression on his face. Alex turned away. In one respect she was glad to see Björn again, but in another she deplored the circumstances that had brought them together. He was even more handsome than she recalled; divested of both his overcoat and jacket the lean strength of his body was evident through the thin silk shirt. Muscles rippled against the fine material and a faint shadow of hairs gave a blueish hue to the front of his shirt. Alex felt an insane desire to feel his strength beneath her hands, to run her fingers through the fine, dark hair curling closely to his well-shaped head.

When Jón offered her a glass of *brennivin* she accepted eagerly, grateful for the diversion. Björn awoke senses in her she did not know existed. It was crazy! She crossed to the window and looked out at the well kept garden and the lake beyond over which glided Arctic terns. In the distance the majestic slopes of Mount Esja added to the grandeur of the scene. She jumped violently as Björn's voice sounded close to her ear, and almost spilled the wine in her agitation.

'Look, it's not my fault it happened like this. I know how you feel about me, but there's no need to make it so evident.'

Glancing at him, Alex realised that he had mistaken her withdrawal as a token of dislike. Maybe it was best if he thought that way—if he knew how she felt what would he think? That she threw herself at every man she met? The idea was ludicrous, yet how else could he interpret her reaction? He had given her no encouragement, no reason at all to feel the way she did. It was something that had happened as suddenly and unpredictably as a summer thunderstorm, but unlike a storm which dies away within a few hours, leaving the earth clean and refreshed, Alex was left with a bitter-sweet mixture of longing and regret, of love and despair. She knew that right now, this minute, she ought to thrust all feelings for this man out of her mind before they had a chance to develop. She might have succeeded had he not turned up again so unexpectedly, but his nearness was like a drug, desirable but dangerous, intoxicating, exhilarating.

He waited for her reply, calmly sipping his lager and watching the conflicting emotions cross her face. For a moment Helga and Jón were forgotten. They were alone.

'I'm sorry,' Alex tilted her head to see him more clearly, 'I didn't mean to be rude. It was a shock seeing you here. I felt—surprised and confused.'

'I know I've given you every reason to dislike me,' his voice was soft, pleading, 'but Helga and Jón are old friends of mine—I don't see them very often, and I don't want to offend them. Couldn't you pretend to like me—just for this evening?'

How could she resist when he looked and spoke to her like that? It would be so easy to forget the type of man he was. The stern, hard businessman who didn't believe in Women's Lib. Deliberately she pushed this side of his character to the back of her mind. If he wanted her friendship he should have it.

One evening could do no harm, and then afterwards she would banish him from her thoughts.

It shouldn't be too difficult. Once the holiday season began it was unlikely their paths would cross. So she smiled; a warm, friendly smile which caused little green lights to dance in her eyes and which drew a surprising response from her companion. He stiffened and frowned before returning an equally cordial smile.

'That's better,' he said, 'I'm sure it wasn't too difficult.' His voice sounded different, as though he held it under careful control—which was ridiculous. Why should he need to restrain his feelings when it was Alex herself who had this problem? She was not allowed to puzzle over this question, though, for Helga asked Björn a question that drew them both back into the centre of the room.

Conversation after that became lively and entertaining, and the evening flew by as if on winged heels. Alex was amazed when Björn announced that he must leave and experienced a pang of sorrow at the thought that she might never see him again. He had shown a charming side to his nature which both intrigued and further excited her.

The insistent ringing of the telephone at the same time as Helga went to fetch Björn's coat called Jón from the room. It was the first time they had been alone during the evening, and the first time he had asked any questions about her future.

'Have you been successful in finding another job?'

Alex shook her head. 'Afraid not. But I've not given up hope.'

He studied his nails for a second as if wondering how to frame his next question, and when at last it came it took Alex by surprise.

'I don't quite know how to put this; but as I've had no success either in finding anyone suitable to act as courier, and as my tour starts tomorrow, I wondered whether you'd agree to taking the job—just for this one trip, of course?'

CHAPTER TWO

'YOU'RE not serious?' Alex looked at Björn in astonishment. 'You were quick enough to point out that this was no job for a woman, what makes you think I'll work for you now?' Her instinct was to accept, but remembrance of his attitude at the airport triggered off a quick spark of annoyance.

'I thought that as a friend you might help me out.' He looked almost humble, making Alex realise how hard it must be to appeal like this. He did not seem the type to swallow pride easily, and she felt an instant sympathy. But she did not show it. Instead she said:

'You're no friend of mine. Have you forgotten this is a truce purely to satisfy Helga and Jón? As far as I'm concerned you're the sort of man from whom I'm trying to escape. If I agree to work with you I can foresee nothing but trouble. Our opinions are too diverse.'

He frowned at that. 'You surprise me. I thought you'd jump at the chance of the job—albeit a temporary one. It won't be easy to find work elsewhere, or do you intend to take advantage of these good folks and get yourself a free holiday into the bargain?'

'How dare you speak to me like that!' His insinuation was all too clear. 'It may interest you to know that I am by no means short of money. Helga and Jón are my friends, I have no intention of sponging off them. I merely decided to take a job as I felt I would be doing more good to society than by sitting at home doing nothing.'

'I see,' he said, though by the cynical quirk of his eyebrow Alex was perfectly sure that he didn't understand. 'So there's no point in pursuing the matter further. I must try and solve my problem some other way.'

He looked worried, and Alex immediately regretted her hastily spoken words. If she admitted the truth, she would like nothing better than to work alongside this handsome Icelander; there would be conflict, of that she had no doubt, but to be near him would more than compensate for such trials.

Björn ran his fingers through his hair agitatedly, and Alex wondered whether it was not too late to change her mind. There was no time for him to find anyone else, and he would be stuck unless she agreed to help out.

She cleared her throat. 'Er—*Herra* Einarsson—Björn—perhaps I will take the job after all.'

His head shot up and he eyed her suspiciously. 'Why? What's made you change your mind?'

She eyed him steadily. It wouldn't do to let him know that she felt sorry for him. 'Put it down to a woman's prerogative. Or is that something else with which you don't agree?'

'I don't seem to have much choice,' he smiled grimly. 'I'm grateful to you, Alexandra. Let's hope I don't regret my decision.'

Again he had given that peculiar personal sound to her name which set her pulses racing. No one else said it in just that same way. It could be because of his Icelandic accent, but it was like a compliment— whether intended or not.

'I'll do my best.' Her voice was husky with emotion, but Björn seemed not to notice. Now that the matter was settled he had risen and was impatient to leave.

'The first party arrives midday tomorrow. I'd like you to be at my headquarters at about nine to help with the packing and checking of equipment. You know where it is?'

Alex nodded. 'I have a good idea—and, Björn, I'll do my best not to let you down.'

'I'm sure you will,' he said drily, 'it's whether your best is good enough that I'm worried about. It's against my better judgment to offer you this job, but beggars can't be choosers, as the saying goes. If anything happens I have only myself to blame.'

'Are you always so pessimistic?' asked Alex, trying hard not to show how his contempt irritated her. 'Don't you ever stop to think that people might be more capable than you give them credit for?'

He smiled cynically. 'Life has taught me that it isn't always wise to follow one's own instincts. They can be misleading.'

'And what were your first reactions as far as I was concerned?' she demanded.

The corners of his mouth quirked. 'I prefer not to tell you—at least not at the moment.'

'Why? Is it so bad that you're afraid I might refuse to help you after all?'

'I guess you might at that.'

Alex was too annoyed to notice the twinkle in his eyes, and as Helga returned at that moment the conversation ended.

Both Helga and her husband were pleased to hear that Alex was to be Björn's courier after all. 'At least I know you'll be well looked after,' said the older woman. 'Björn's a perfect gentleman and will make sure that nothing happens to you.'

'You sound very confident,' replied Alex, 'I wish I felt the same. I know Björn didn't really want to give me this job and he'll watch me like a hawk. I hope I don't do anything stupid.'

It was with some trepidation that Alex entered the premises of Björn Einarsson Travel the next morning, and her fears were not dispelled by the curt greeting of her employer. He gave her no more than a cursory good morning before thrusting a set of papers into her hand and telling her to check the equipment as it was stowed away. It hurt that he should treat her like this and only increased her nervousness. She had been so looking forward to working alongside Björn.

She had lain awake far into the night thinking about this man who had aroused her senses in a way no other man had. Whether the attraction was purely physical she had no way of knowing; all she did know was that Björn Einarsson was the most irresistible man she had ever met. His dark charm had completely enslaved her and the thought of being in his company for the next fourteen days was an ecstasy beyond belief. Now she felt as deflated as a burst balloon. At least he could have offered some encouraging advice! He knew that she had never done a job of this sort, or any other type of work for that matter. Why then did he have to treat her as though her being there was a mere formality? She felt like a cog in a wheel—no more, no less.

Nevertheless she carried out her job conscientiously and when the last tent, the last knife, fork and spoon, had been stowed, and all items ticked off on the sheets, she experienced a feeling of satisfaction at a job well done.

When Björn smiled and suggested she make them both a cup of coffee she immediately forgot the animosity he had aroused and cheerfully agreed. Now that the job was over he appeared more relaxed and Alex was surprised by her own equally fluent change of mood. It was strange how she could easily adapt herself to his frame of mind and forget her earlier disappointment—it seemed he had only to smile and she was completely enslaved. She knew she ought to try and think of him purely as her employer, he had made it clear that she meant nothing to him. Yet there was an indefinable something that made her think of him as someone different. A man to be desired—a man to love.

Sighing at her own thoughts, Alex took their coffee into the room he used as an office. It was sparsely furnished with a desk and chairs, and Björn had his feet up on the desk and a dossier of papers in his hand.

'We'll take a steady ride out once we've finished here. Perhaps you'd like to see this map of our route. If there are any questions you wish to ask, please don't hesitate.'

After a brief glance Alex knew that she was familiar with all the places, and would have no difficulty in introducing their visitors to the delights of each sector of the country.

Glancing covertly at Björn, she saw that he was completely immersed in the papers in front of him, and she took the opportunity to study his face. The heavy lids shut out the smoke-grey eyes, but she had no difficulty in remembering their smouldering intensity. His lips in repose were full and well shaped, and Alex could not help but wonder what it would feel like to be kissed by him. She closed her eyes and could feel them light and gentle against her own, becoming more demanding as he felt no resistance. His voice brought her sharply back to reality.

'Did you not sleep well last night, Alexandra?'

Alex jumped and looked at him wide-eyed, thankful that he could not read her thoughts. 'I'm sorry, I—I was thinking.'

He frowned. 'The job won't be too much for you? You're sure about it? Please tell me now, before it's too late.'

'It's not the job,' she assured him hastily, 'I—I was thinking of something else.'

'If it's the boy-friend who put that blissful expression on to your face, then I suggest you forget him. There will be no time in this job for romancing.'

His voice was critical, causing Alex to retort, 'I have no boy-friend. At least—that is—I did have, but not any longer.' Why she bothered to explain she did not know, except that her intrinsic honesty forbade her to do otherwise. At least it would stop him from suspecting that he was the person at the other end of her thoughts! She went hot at the mere idea of him guessing. How amusing he would find it that Alex Constantine thought herself to be in love with him. Adolescent infatuation was what he would term it, decided Alex. She must be more careful in future.

'I see. The big row, eh? That explains why you want to get away from England. I just hope that he doesn't decide to come over here and take you back. Perhaps I ought to insist you sign a contract—to safeguard my own interests?'

'I'll sign if you like, Herra Einarsson,' said Alex tightly, 'but you have my word that I shan't fail you. After all, it's only for two weeks, unless you decide to let me stay on for the season after all.'

He eyed her steadily. 'That will depend on how well you do this trip. Don't forget I have no faith in you, so it will be up to you to prove yourself.'

'You certainly don't give me any encouragement,' Alex could not help retorting. 'Maybe I should ask whether you've changed *your* mind? Are you sure you want me to accompany you?'

Swiftly he stabbed out his cigarette. His actions were tempered with annoyance and Alex caught a steely glint in his eyes. 'I do not appear to have any alternative.' He rose suddenly. 'If you've finished your coffee we'll go.' And he marched out of the room, giving her no alternative but to follow.

The journey to Keflavik was accomplished in silence. Björn's face was set into grim lines and he appeared deep in thought. Once or twice Alex went to speak, then changed her mind for fear of a rebuff. This first tour was as much an experiment for Björn as it was for herself and it would have been so much better had they begun on friendly terms.

She slanted a glance in his direction, noting the taut lines of his mouth and the way his hands were clenched on the wheel as though it were a life line. She hoped above everything else that this venture would be a success, and had it not been for her impulsively-spoken words a few minutes earlier, they could even now have been discussing the tour; planning what they would do and speculating on the members of the party. By coincidence this first group was from England, so there would be no difficulty as far as language was concerned.

It was imperative for Alex's own peace of mind that she proved to be a successful courier, even if only to squash Björn's theory that this job was not suitable for a woman. Other women held posts as couriers, so why not her? Just because she didn't look the part it didn't mean that she wasn't. And being hostile with Björn wouldn't help. She took a deep breath.

'I'm sorry—I shouldn't have spoken to you like that.'

For one moment she thought he hadn't heard. Not by so much as the bat of an eyelid did he give any indication of hearing her apology. She was about to speak again when he looked across quickly, acknowledging her words by a slight nod of his head. That was all.

They were nearing the airport now, and Alex gave a mental shrug. If he didn't want to speak there wasn't much she could do about it. But the sting of tears beneath her eyelids gave away the fact that his indifference hurt. How much easier her job would be with his approval and help! She blinked away the tears and gathered up her bag preparatory to leaving the bus.

'For heaven's sake you're not crying?' Björn had halted the bus and turned to face her. 'That's all I need to convince me I've made a mistake.'

'Of course not.' Alex glared at him defiantly. 'I have something in my eye, that's all,' dabbing her face with a handkerchief. She had hoped he wouldn't notice her distress; he had paid no attention to her throughout the journey, so it seemed probable that he wouldn't notice now. But she had said the wrong thing. Before she knew what was happening Björn had slid across and was on the seat beside her, a snowy white handkerchief at the ready. 'Here, let me look. I know how painful it can be.'

Dumbly Alex allowed him to rest her head back against the seat and peer into the offending eye. His nearness made her feel dizzy and it was all she could do to stop herself putting out a hand to touch his face. Tracing the fine lines round his eyes, smoothing the frown from his forehead. The sharp, pungent odour of after-shave stimulated her senses and she felt her fingernails digging into the palms of her hands in an endeavour to control her racing pulses. She looked deep into his eyes, saw reflected there a miniaturised image of her own face, and blinked quickly, involuntarily. 'I—I think it's gone now,' she said, willing him to move. She was finding it difficult to breathe evenly, and was sure he must notice.

He eased himself away a few inches, but his arm remained on the seat behind her head. 'Your tears have probably washed it away,' he said. 'I can't see anything, unless it's beneath the lid. Would you like me to——?'

'Oh, no, it's all right now. Hadn't we better go?' She watched him apprehensively, and was relieved when he pulled his big frame up from the seat and opened the door.

It was not until she had seen Björn glance three times at his watch that she realised he too was nervous about the forthcoming tour, and wished she could think of something comforting to say. If he had treated her differently it would have been so easy to talk to him, but as it was she was afraid of invoking further wrath by saying the wrong thing. It wasn't a very good beginning to the tour, but what could she do about it, except hope that things would sort themselves out? Once he saw how efficiently she was coping, maybe his attitude towards her would change.

He looked again at his watch—a magnificent gold affair that looked every pound of what it had cost— and soon after that the plane arrived. Before long a steady stream of people emerged through Customs. As soon as they were all assembled and checked against Alex's list and their luggage stowed in the back of the bus, they set off on the return trip to Reykjavik, and the camping site by the outdoor swimming pool in the eastern sector.

This time Alex did not have to sit up front and endure Björn's interminable silence. She mingled with the passengers, introducing herself and answering the many questions put to her. By the time they reached their destination she had a good mental picture of their travelling companions for the next two weeks.

There were Valerie and Brian Danks, on honeymoon and entirely wrapped up in each other's company; Vera and Harry Griffin—she didn't like them much—he was a travelling salesman and boasted of his frequent trips to this country. To hear him talk you would think he knew everything. She intended avoiding him as much as possible, as she could see a strong clash of wills as far as he was concerned.

The oldest couple were a Mr and Mrs Shaw, in

their mid-sixties, and enjoying one last good holiday before settling down to live on their pension. The rest of the party were couples of differing ages, apart from Austin Maddison, a keen geologist who was avid for information on the rock formation and volcanic and glacial phenomena of the island. Alex could not help him much in this direction apart from a general knowledge of the area, but he was a pleasant young man and she had spent several minutes chatting until he felt almost like an old friend. Beside him sat Juliet Devall, who was also travelling alone, and who was something of an enigma to Alex. She was an extremely sophisticated blonde who looked entirely out of context. She had little to say, and Alex had eventually given up try-ing to make conversation. No doubt she would eventually find out exactly why Juliet had chosen to take just such a holiday as this, but for the moment she was a mystery.

At the site the kitchen truck had a meal waiting for the hungry party. All the meals on this tour were very much picnic affairs, with tables set out outside the kitchen truck and the passengers helping themselves to food. For a while Alex could relax, and as she waited her turn Björn came across. 'How's it going? They look a pretty good bunch. Do you think they'll get on well together?'

'I think so,' smiled Alex. 'There's only Harry Griffin who might give us trouble—one of the know-it-all types—he's been here before and is boring everyone with his accounts of the island.'

'So long as his facts are accurate it should ease

your burden,' he replied, 'but I'll keep an eye on him. We don't want anyone getting the wrong impression of my country.'

Alex knew by the way he spoke that he was very proud of Iceland, as indeed he had every right to be. For visitors who had never visited it before the majestic mountains, the rainbow-bridged waterfalls, the spouting geysers and the strange moon-like landscape of the interior were a sight that once seen was never to be forgotten.

'What's the name of the blonde eating alone?' asked Björn next, nodding his head in the direction of Juliet. 'Is she travelling by herself?'

'That's right. I can't quite make her out. Her name's Juliet Devall,' and anticipating his next question, '*Miss* Devall. I hope she doesn't prove a nuisance. She looks the type who prefers all mod cons, and isn't going to like it a bit when she has to rough it.'

'I see. I think I'll have a word with her,' and before Alex could speak again Björn strode over to where Juliet Devall sat, and lowered himself at her side.

Alex knew it was silly, but she felt offended that he should prefer Juliet's company. After all, he was only doing his duty as a good tour operator; but her feelings were hurt and no matter how she tried to ignore them she could not help stealing a glance in their direction every now and then. The fact that he seemed to be getting on well with the elegant blonde didn't help either. And when Björn burst into a roar of laughter at something Juliet said, Alex felt like walking across and slapping the other girl's face. It rankled that he should get on so well with a complete stranger when he treated Alex herself so badly.

Perhaps it was fortunate that Austin Maddison chose that moment to seek her out. 'Mind if I eat with you? You're looking very dejected. Are you worried about the trip?'

Alex smiled. 'Not at all. At least I don't think so. Hang on while I grab some food.' In a few minutes she was back, and they squatted on the grass together. Alex had experienced some pretty bad weather in Iceland and was grateful that this year it looked as though they were in for a good summer. Even as early in the season as the beginning of June it was not too cold, not by Icelandic standards, though the average holidaymaker from Britain might find it decidedly cooler than in his own country. Windcheaters and trousers were worn by all, but in Alex's mind they were fortunate that it was not much colder.

'You were about to tell me what was on your mind,' Austin said, biting into one of the delicious-looking open sandwiches.

'How do you know there's anything bothering me?' asked Alex, startled by this young man's direct attack. He was not quite so tall as Björn, but good-looking in a less positive kind of way. His mid-brown hair was brushed back in what Alex tended to think of as an old-fashioned style compared to the much more unconventional hairdos of the present day, but his hazel eyes were kind and when he smiled his teeth were white and even. He would never treat her with the hostility she had suffered at the hands of her employer, she was sure. His was a kind, considerate nature, in fact—a typical English gentleman.

'You have an open face,' he replied, 'you should learn to guard your feelings more. Is it Mr Einarsson who's bothering you?'

Horrified by the accuracy of his judgment, Alex shook her head. 'Björn? He doesn't worry me. I'll let you into a secret. This is my first trip as courier, and I'm feeling a little nervous.'

'You don't say? I'd never have guessed. The way you chatted to us all on the coach, making us feel at ease and explaining what was in store—it was as though you'd been doing the job for a lifetime. I don't think you need have any fears in that respect.'

'Thanks, Austin, you're a great comfort. I'll know where to come when I'm feeling depressed.'

'It will be my pleasure,' he smiled. 'I say, if this is an example of the sort of food we can expect on this journey I shan't want to go back to my digs in London.'

'You live alone?' she asked.

'That's right, I eat out most of the time or grab a quick sandwich at the pub. My parents live in Sussex. I go home weekends and for holidays.' He chewed a mouthful of smoked salmon appreciatively. 'I certainly never expected anything like this.'

'Björn Einarsson Travel are out to please,' smiled Alex, watching the blissful expression on his face.

'If you have any complaints please report them to the management forthwith.'

'Certainly will,' agreed Austin, 'but I doubt if that will be necessary.'

Unable to resist stealing another glance in Björn's direction, Alex was just in time to see dark disapproval in his face as he turned away. Didn't he like her keeping Austin company?

She looked round at the other holidaymakers—they appeared perfectly content, and by the looks on their faces were finding the food very much to their liking. She couldn't be of any help, there so why the implied criticism? He was doing the same himself, and to all outward appearances enjoying every minute of it. Juliet Devall looked happier than she had since arriving, and from the way she regarded Björn it was clear that he had won himself a friend.

Alex clenched her fists, and then, afraid that Austin with his all-too-discerning eyes might notice her change of mood, said quickly, 'How would you like to fetch us both some coffee? I can assure you it will be as excellent as the food.'

He jumped up willingly, and Alex changed her position so that she had her back to her formidable employer. The less she saw of him with the hateful Juliet Devall, for this was how she was beginning to think of the other woman, the better!

In seconds Austin was back and began an animated conversation on the basalt and palagonite rock formations of Iceland.

'Do you know it's believed that Iceland was once

connected to Greenland and Great Britain?'

'I've heard something of the kind,' agreed Alex, 'but I've never taken much interest in geology.'

'Then you should,' he said eagerly, 'it's far more interesting than anyone thinks. It's generally believed that the basalt formation here is a remnant of a region that at one time connected the three countries together. It's fascinating, and I can't wait to start explorations.'

Alex smiled. He was so wildly enthusiastic she couldn't help but feel interested. 'I can see I'm going to learn a lot more about Iceland's geology before the tour's finished. You just mind you don't wander off and lose yourself, or I'll be to blame.'

'Don't worry, I'll be careful. Do you mind if I go now? I've just remembered something I want to look up.'

'Not at all,' said Alex, but he had gone. She laughed softly to herself and rose, but before she could move away a detaining hand touched her arm.

'I don't want to play the part of the iron master,' Björn's voice sounded close to her ear, 'but do you think it wise to become so friendly with a member of the party?'

'You're a fine one to——' began Alex, then remembering her position and the fact that she was on trial, continued, 'Mr Maddison is travelling alone. If you'd rather I neglected him——'

'That is not the point.' He was in front of her now, his voice softly guarded from the rest of the passengers, but terse enough for Alex to realise that he was annoyed. 'I do not wish you, as courier, to

46

fraternise with any one particular member of my party; you are to be friendly to all, but no more—understand?'

Alex bit back the hasty retort that he had behaved in a similar manner, and nodded. 'I'll do my best, but it will be impossible not to give him more of my time than the others.'

'And Miss Devall—don't forget she's on her own too. You'll give her special attention? She's feeling very lonely at the moment.'

I'm not surprised, thought Alex. She ought to have had more sense than to come. 'I'll try, though I don't expect much success. She's not exactly my type, and might resent me trying to push my friendship on her. Perhaps she and Austin might get together—that would solve all our problems.'

'I doubt it,' he said shortly, and Alex was surprised by the decisive way in which he had said those words.

'You seem very sure. Have you found out why she came?'

'Why should there be a reason—except the same one as the others? She wanted a holiday in Iceland and thought my tour looked the most attractive, that's all.' He sounded curt.

'I'm surprised,' replied Alex, 'but if that's what she's told you——'

'She has, and I have no reason to believe otherwise. Now, if you'd like to announce the next item on the itinerary, I'd be much obliged.'

His face brooked no refusal. Fuming inwardly, Alex assumed what she hoped was a pleasant smile and announced to the party that there would now be a conducted tour round Reykjavik. They could, if they wished, explore the city for themselves so long as they were back at the camp reasonably early. Tea would be available from five o'clock onwards, and afterwards the tents would be erected for their first night in Iceland.

It worked out that all of the holidaymakers preferred to discover what Reykjavik had to offer for themselves. Austin invited Alex to join him, but in view of Björn's earlier comments she declined, much as she would have liked to go. Instead Austin went alone, leaving Alex and Björn—and Juliet.

'I've seen Reykjavik,' she admitted when Björn questioned her decision.

'I wasn't aware you'd visited Iceland before,' he said.

She tossed her head in a provocative gesture. 'Many times—though I've always stayed in first-class hotels, of course, never anything like this.'

'Then why have you come?' The words were out before Alex could stop them.

'You might say to try and widen my horizons,' declared the other girl. 'It does us all good to have a change at some time or other.'

'Then I hope you find your holiday very enjoyable,' replied Alex politely, and to Björn, who looked far from pleased with her, 'If there's nothing further I can do, I think I'll go into Reykjavik myself.'

She needed to get away from this haughty young woman who showed every sign of being attracted to

Björn. Why else would she decide to stay behind? It hurt more than Alex cared to admit to see the two of them together, hence her decision to go into Reykjavik after all. She would call in and see Helga; the older woman's soothing influence would soon restore her peace of mind.

It took only a few minutes to reach the house. Jón was out, but Helga welcomed her warmly. 'This is a surprise,' she said, 'back so soon—you haven't given up the job already?'

Alex laughed at her worried expression. 'Of course not. I have time to spare while the visitors are looking over the city, so I decided to come and see you. It seems ages since I left this morning.'

'Do you think you're going to like the job?' Helga put away her knitting and filled the kettle for the inevitable cup of coffee.

'Yes and no.' Alex paused, considering her reply. 'On the whole they seem a good crowd, except for one bitch of a woman who's after Björn already. I hate her!'

'Them's fighting words,' laughed Helga, 'but I shouldn't worry too much. Björn's far too sensible to allow a pretty blonde go to his head.'

Alex lifted her brows in surprise. 'How do you know she's a blonde?'

'Isn't the other woman always fair? Especially if one's dark. You've fallen for him yourself, haven't you?'

Alex nodded. 'Is it so obvious? Please don't tell him. He hasn't a very good opinion of me without adding love to his problems.'

'I shouldn't be too sure about that,' said Helga wisely. 'When you two were here together last night, I gained the impression that he liked you more than just a little.'

'If he does he has a funny way of showing it,' returned Alex hotly. 'He does nothing but shout at me. I shall be a nervous wreck by the end of the trip if I'm not careful!'

The water boiled and Helga proceeded to fill the coffee pot, saying as she did so, 'I'd willingly stake my life savings that that man's fond of you. He probably treats you like he does because he's worried about his venture and doesn't want anything to go wrong.'

'I wish I could believe you, Helga. I've never met a man quite like him before.' Alex gazed into space for a second. 'If you're right—although I very much doubt it—by the time the tour has ended, and if it's a success, we should be good friends.'

'Of course you will, love, you mark my words. Now, drink your coffee while it's hot. I'd planned a trip to the shops—would you like to come?'

'Love to. I needn't be back until five.'

It was half-past four when they returned to Helga's house. 'Just right,' observed Alex, 'a steady walk back and I should be there before any of our holidaymakers return.'

At that moment the telephone rang. She followed Helga out into the hall, preparatory to leaving, but rushed forward when she saw her friend's stricken face, guiding her to the nearest chair. 'What is it? What's the matter?'

'It's Jón, he's had an accident.' Helga's voice was lifeless. 'He's in hospital. I must go to him.'

Alex knew that she could not let her down, even though time was against her. 'I'll call a taxi. Which hospital is he in?'

'The National. They said he's critical.' Tears squeezed from the woman's eyes, and Alex knew that if anything happened to Jón it would be the end for Helga. They lived for each other, these two, and one without the other would be like flowers without rain.

Quickly now, Alex dialled for the taxi, and while they waited poured Helga a glass of whisky, which helped to restore the colour to her cheeks.

'I'm sure Jón will be all right,' encouraged Alex, 'he has a good constitution. It will take more than a little accident to keep him down. What happened exactly?'

'A hit-and-run driver, as far as I could make out,' wept Helga. 'Perhaps we'll find out more when we get there.'

Within minutes the taxi arrived and soon they were at the hospital. They were allowed straight in to see Jón. His head was swathed in bandages and he was unconscious. Alex had never seen Helga look so upset, and she led her away before she broke down altogether. 'He'll be all right, I'm sure,' she consoled.

The doctor took them into his room. 'Don't worry, Frú Pétursdóttir, we're doing all we can for your husband, and you can stay here tonight. We're not sure how long it will be before he comes round, but I expect you'd like to be here when he does?'

'Thank you, doctor. How did it happen?'

'We're not really sure. One witness said that a car struck your husband as he was crossing the road, and another—well, why don't we wait until he can tell us himself what happened? It's purely guesswork at the moment.'

Alex accompanied Helga to her room. It was fortunate they weren't busy, for otherwise Alex did not see how she could have left Helga at home by herself. There was no guessing what she might do. A nurse brought in a sedative and then it was Helga herself who suggested that Alex ought to go.

'Whatever will Björn think, you being so late like this? You must tell him what happened.'

'Don't you worry, Helga dear. I don't suppose there was much I could do at the camp. I'll phone you tomorrow. I do wish I could stay with you.'

Helga squeezed her hand. 'Now it's my turn to tell you not to worry! I'll be all right here. You go and get on with your job.'

'Goodbye, Helga. I'll keep in touch.' There were tears in Alex's eyes as she waved farewell, but once out of sight she dashed along the corridor and phoned yet again for a taxi. It was not far to the field where they camped, but every minute now seemed vital. Although her delay could not be helped she knew that Björn was not going to be very pleased.

She was right. Almost before she had set foot on the camp he was there, a thunderous expression darkening his face. 'Where the devil do you think you've been?'

'I'm sorry—I was with Helga at——'

52

'And you conveniently forgot the time? Well, let me tell you, young woman, the very next time this happens you will be dismissed, whether it's in the middle of the interior or at the top of a glacier, I don't care. I will not tolerate bad time-keeping. Now, will you go and help Mr and Mrs Shaw put up their tent? I suppose you do know how to do it, or is that another of your feminine weaknesses?'

Alex glared back at him, too annoyed now to speak up in her own defence. Let him think what he liked. What did it matter? 'I know,' she said tightly. 'I'm not entirely incapable, even if you'd like to think me so,' and she turned sharply away, leaving him to stare after her.

CHAPTER THREE

ALEX woke early the next morning and lay staring for a few minutes at the orange canvas overhead, tugging her sleeping bag more tightly round her neck as the cold morning air touched her skin.

Today the tour started in earnest. Nothing must go wrong. She could not risk incurring Björn's wrath again or she would be out of a job. Yesterday evening he had hidden his displeasure in front of the holidaymakers, but Alex had felt his anger and as a result had been unusually on edge.

Austin, noticing her agitation, had given her a hand with the Shaws' tent. Alex had wanted to refuse his help, as she was sure Björn would think she had been lying and was unsure of how to do the job, but as her fingers seemed all thumbs and the erection would have taken twice as long by herself, she gratefully accepted.

'Is there anything the matter?' Austin queried in concern. 'You look very upset.'

Alex shook her head. 'I'm worried about a friend of mine who was knocked down by a car this afternoon. He's still unconscious.' She preferred not to mention that it was Björn who had upset her. Had she been an ordinary employee she would not have hesitated to stick up for herself, but loving him as she did, it was impossible to remain unaffected by his attitude. All she could do was try and see that nothing else happened to annoy him.

'I'm sorry to hear that,' said Austin. 'I can understand how you feel, especially knowing you won't be able to visit him. But are you sure that that's all? Björn hasn't been on to you, has he? He looked pretty mad earlier on.'

'He did say a few words,' admitted Alex, 'but I suppose he had every right to be angry. He's taken me on as courier and I'm supposed to be reliable— not turn up late the very first day.' Why she was bothering to defend Björn after the way he had spoken to her she did not know, but she could not bring herself to say anything bad about him, even if she did think it sometimes.

'But you couldn't help it. Not when something like that happened. I think he's being unreasonable.

It's funny, I didn't think he was like that—he seems a decent sort of chap.'

Alex's smile was ironical. 'I'm on trial, don't forget.'

'I'd forgotten,' he admitted, 'but I shouldn't worry too much. You seem pretty capable to me, and conscientious, which is more than can be said for a lot of young people.'

'Thanks for the compliment, but it doesn't help the way Björn feels.'

Austin touched her arm. 'You have me to back you up now. If I can be of any help just say the word.'

As she unzipped her sleeping bag, Alex recalled Austin's words, and although she hoped never to need his help it was nice to know that she had someone to whom she could turn if things got difficult. Their first stop today was Hveragerdi, situated in an active hot spring area, which would give their visitors their first sight of hot springs and, if they were lucky, an eruption of one of the geysers.

Eager to make a good start, Alex pulled on her trousers and sweater and dashed across to the washroom. Soon she was feeling refreshed and ready to face whatever the day had to offer. By now the camp was alive with activity, tents were being pulled down and stowed into the bus and the appetising smell of breakfast made her feel hungry.

Austin was helping the Shaws with their tent, and as everyone else seemed to be managing for themselves she crossed to the kitchen truck to see whether she could be of any help in that direction.

She had not noticed Björn standing there, discussing the day's menu with Maggie, the Scottish cook, who had married an Icelander. Perhaps if she had she might not have been so eager to offer help.

He nodded a formal greeting. 'Good morning. I trust you're all ready. You've checked the route we are taking today?'

If Alex hoped he had relented she was disappointed. There was nothing in either the way he spoke or looked to indicate that he had forgiven her. It was a disheartening prospect to think that he might treat her in this unfriendly manner for the whole of the tour, when she had been so looking forward to his company; but, determined not to let him see how unhappy he had made her, Alex smiled cheerfully, and said:

'Good morning, Herra Einarsson, Maggie. Yes, I'm perfectly familiar with the ground we're covering. I'm glad the weather's good, it will make the holiday so much more enjoyable for our visitors.'

'Don't be too optimistic,' grunted Björn. 'Anything can happen before the two weeks are up,' and murmuring an excuse he moved away.

Alex watched, a tiny frown of annoyance on her brow, as she saw him stop and give Juliet a helping hand with her tent. The girl seemed to know what she was doing, so Alex could not quite see the idea behind his offer of assistance, unless he was as smitten with her as she was with him. It was an idea which had not previously occurred to Alex, and one that she didn't very much like. She turned away. It was none of her business what he chose to do—

except that she did not wish to see him make a fool of himself.

Over breakfast everyone discussed what sort of night they had spent, and some of them expressed their preference for a proper bed. Harry Griffin in particular was not slow to complain about his discomfort, but his wife, Vera, soon dispelled this story by declaring that he had fallen asleep as soon as the zip was fastened round his sleeping bag and she had been afraid that his snores would wake the rest of the camp.

Austin brought his breakfast over to Alex once again. 'Mind if I join you?' he asked, and as Björn was nowhere in sight—not that it mattered what he thought, declared Alex to herself—she nodded agreement.

'I trust you had a good night?'

'Slept like a log,' he said emphatically. 'And you? You look, if I may say so, a little jaded this morning.'

'I didn't sleep too badly,' admitted Alex, 'but it's been a long time since I did any camping, when I was a Girl Guide, in fact, and I didn't realise the tents would be so small. It's a good job I don't suffer from claustrophobia—and nor do any of these other people.'

'I should think that's the least of your worries,' smiled Austin. 'Once this good clean Icelandic air gets into their lungs they'll crawl into their tents and know nothing more until it's time to get up.' He inhaled deeply, filling his lungs and letting it go in one swift breath. 'Wonderful—so unpolluted. Do you know that even the drinking water is so pure here that it can be used instead of distilled water in car batteries?'

Alex laughed and nodded. 'So I believe! You know an awful lot about this country, considering you've never been here before.'

He tapped his temple. 'It's all up here. I've studied Iceland for months, and now I'm hoping to put my theory into practice.'

'Don't let Björn hear you say that. or he'll be offering you my job.'

Alex meant this as a joke, but Austin became suddenly serious at her words. 'I wish you wouldn't let that man bother you so much. Don't you think that perhaps you're imagining a lot of it because you're unsure of yourself?'

Alex shrugged. 'I'd like to think you're right, but'—she paused and took another mouthful of porridge—'there are so many times when he could be nice to me but isn't.'

'He's a man with a lot of responsibility,' pondered Austin. 'It's natural he feels a bit apprehensive. He probably doesn't even know he hurts your feelings.'

Sensing that Austin would never completely see her side of the argument, Alex allowed the matter to drop. They finished their meal in a companionable silence and it was not until she was taking her dishes back to the kitchen that she saw Björn. He sat on a boulder at the side of the truck and had been hidden from view. But it was clear that he had seen her, and he made no attempt to hide the fact that he disapproved. Alex sighed, and deliberately avoided going near him. She had no wish to be further censured.

After helping clear away Alex took the opportunity to go and phone the hospital. She was relieved to hear that Jón had improved during the night, and she didn't feel so bad now about leaving Helga on her own.

Soon everyone was ready and they set off on the first stage of their journey. Alex drew the attention of the passengers to the heather and lava fields over which they drove, determinedly making use of all her knowledge to make the journey as interesting as possible for the members of the party whose first visit this was to Iceland.

'We shall soon be approaching Hveragerdi,' she announced. 'This is a hot spring area, as indicated by its name—*Hver* means hot spring. You will find exotic flowers and fruit on sale, grown in greenhouses heated by this unique natural heat.'

A murmur of interest ran through her audience and heads were craned in order to be the first to see the vapour-covered slopes and the powerful steam jets which were emitted from time to time from the boreholes.

Björn slanted a glance in her direction. 'If you carry on like that I can see I shall have nothing to worry about.'

She smiled, suddenly warmed by his praise. It was funny how a few kind words could make her forget his ungraciousness, or how easily a few hard words hurt! 'Thank you. I've travelled this route many times with my grandfather, it's almost like coming home.'

'You speak as though you'd like to live here. Is that your intention, or does your young man want to keep you in England?' He kept his eyes on the road as he spoke, so that Alex was unable to read his expression.

'I told you before that I have no boy-friend. It's over—finished. As far as living here is concerned, I wouldn't mind with——' She cut short her sentence. She had been about to say with the right man, but could imagine his ironic humour if she were to make such a statement. '—If I could find suitable accommodation,' she finished lamely.

'It shouldn't be too difficult to find an apartment. Let me know when the tour's over if you're still interested, and I'll see what I can do.'

Alex shot him a suspicious look. This was the first time he had offered her help of any sort, and it didn't quite add up with the mental picture she had built of him. 'That's very kind of you,' she said politely, 'I'll certainly keep it in mind.'

They had reached Hveragerdi by this time and the passengers were eager to leave the bus and explore for themselves the curious phenomena of this geothermal area. She saw Austin march off determinedly and smiled to herself. Juliet too, in her red anorak and trousers, had wandered away with the rest of the party and Alex was left alone with Björn. He leaned nonchalantly against the front of the bus, its once gleaming white-and-green paintwork already sullied by the dust of the Icelandic roads. He lighted a cigarette and drew on it appreciatively, his eyes narrowed against the morning sun. 'So far so good,' he drawled.

He appeared to be in an unusually affable mood, but Alex was still wary about speaking to him. She seemed to make a habit of rubbing him up the wrong way, so she smiled and nodded and walked away a few steps, keeping a watchful eye on the party under her care.

'Alexandra.' His voice reached her softly. 'Did you really mean it—about staying here?'

Surprised by his question, Alex returned to his side, a slight frown creasing her brow. 'Yes, but why do you ask? Do you consider it unwise?'

He studied the tip of his cigarette. 'To a certain extent, yes. It would be lonely, for one thing, and a girl alone is—well—vulnerable. It could lead to all sorts of unsavoury situations.'

Alex stiffened. 'Are you insinuating that I would allow disreputable characters into my rooms?'

He quirked an eyebrow. 'You might not know, until it was too late. Living with your grandfather can't have given you much experience of human nature and there are plenty of dubious people about.'

'I should certainly be careful who I invited,' replied Alex evenly, 'probably only Helga and Jón to begin with. After all, as you say, there's no one else I can trust.' His eyes narrowed at this intentional thrust, but for once she didn't care. Not satisfied with declaring her unsuitable for the job, he had now added further insult to injury by assuming she was naïve in the ways of men! 'But you don't have to worry,' she continued, 'I assure you I'm quite capable of looking after myself.'

'Let's hope you're right.' He flicked his cigarette to the floor and ground the butt beneath his heel.

Alex had the feeling that he was taking vengeance out on his filter tip instead of on her, but deliberately kept her tone light. 'If you don't mind I'd like to go and buy some of the delicious fruit sold here before everyone returns.'

'Good idea,' was his surprising reply, 'I'll come with you.'

It had been Alex's intention to get away from Björn and his caustic comments, but she couldn't very well say so, and she was forced to walk beside him until they reached the point where the fruit and flowers were on sale.

They were waiting to be served when suddenly a scarlet-clad figure pushed her unceremoniously to one side. 'Björn! I expected you to come with us. I've been looking for you everywhere.'

'Juliet!' The warmth on his face was unmistakable and Alex felt as though a cold hand clutched her heart. She turned away, disillusioned and disappointed. Maybe he had not been exactly friendly, but at least he had sought her company; now it was obvious where his preference lay. It was only for the sake of convention that he had not followed Juliet out to the hot spring area. Sadly she returned to the bus, the brilliance of the day dimmed.

Much as she tried to push from her mind the fact that her employer meant more to her than any other man, it was difficult in such circumstances not to feel hurt, resentful even. It was not in Alex's make-up to bear ill-will, but Juliet Devall had appeared like an enemy in the camp, and as such Alex disliked her. She clearly intended to let nothing stand in her way in her pursuit of Björn and he, on the other hand, was evidently impressed. It was plain that some motive lay behind the blonde girl making this trip, and that without the presence of such an attractive man as their Icelandic host she would be bored to tears. But what was her reason? Alex couldn't even begin to guess.

How long she sat there she did not know, but the sound of voices suddenly roused her. The passengers were returning. Gradually the bus filled and conversation centred round the morning's activities. Austin, the last to board, gave her a questioning look, but if he saw anything amiss he said nothing, for which Alex was grateful. It would not do for the holidaymakers to see their courier upset. She was their guide, bright and cheerful and eager to be of service at all times. She answered pleasantly the many questions that were now thrust at her, and failed to notice the return of Juliet and Björn. It was not until he inquired whether all the passengers were present that she realised he was there.

She nodded, unable to bring herself to face him, but Juliet, looking as blissful as a cat who has stolen the cream, slanted an unmistakably triumphant look in Alex's direction. *She knows how I feel*, thought Alex in distress. *I really must try to hide my feelings.*

For the next part of their journey she purposely

dimissed Björn from her mind, concentrating instead on the wonderful views this part of the island had to offer. They passed through the farming communities of Selfoss and Hella, and she pointed out the famous volcano, Mount Hekla, in the distance.

Böjrn drove silently and steadily, pausing occasionally to give his passengers opportunity to appreciate the breathtaking views of southern Iceland. Lunch was an uneventful occasion and Alex began to feel that the holiday was at last settling down to a peaceful relationship between passengers and crew.

Their destination for the night was the picturesque Thórsmörk valley. In order to reach this isolated glade the turbulent glacial Markarfljót river had to be crossed, and all faces were pressed to the windows as they moved through the rapidly flowing waters. It was so deep in places that an awed silence fell over the passengers, and Alex knew they wondered whether the bus would make it.

A sudden brash voice from the rear caused her to look round sharply.

'Say, driver, shouldn't we have crossed this river earlier in the day?' It was Harry Griffin, making his way towards the front of the vehicle.

The peaceful interlude was over. Alex, eyeing him warily, hoped he wasn't out to cause trouble and wondered what Björn's reaction would be. She herself had suffered enough from his sharp tongue to know what it felt like to be cut down to size. Surprisingly enough, to Alex at least, Björn spoke quietly and evenly.

'I think it would be safe to say that I know what

I'm doing.' His eyes flickered into the mirror, leaving the foaming waters for a second or two. 'If you wouldn't mind resuming your seat, Mr—er—Griffin.'

The attention of the whole coach was now focused on the round, red face of the irate passenger.

'I tell you, folks,' he drawled, ignoring Björn's request, 'this guy's mad. Everyone knows that on a sunny day like this the best time to cross one of these rivers is at dawn.'

Alex knew that what he said was true, but she trusted Björn implicitly. If it wasn't safe for them to cross he wouldn't attempt it.

'Please, Mr Griffin——' She rose and caught his arm. 'Mr Einarsson is fully experienced in these conditions. There's nothing at all to worry about. Please sit down—you're upsetting the rest of the passengers.'

She could see by their expressions that several people were ready to believe Harry Griffin. It was strange the way people reacted to situations like this; normally placid individuals could become quite hysterical if they thought, no matter how wrongly, that their lives were in danger. She must try and stop this aggravating man before he did any more damage.

But before she could speak again he pushed her unceremoniously out of the way. Her ankle twisted awkwardly beneath her as she fell, but ignoring the sudden pain, Alex fixed her attention on Harry.

'For those of you who don't know,' he continued, apparently enjoying the sensation he had caused, 'on a day like today the melted water increases and these rivers swell until they become damn near impassable by late afternoon.' He paused to ensure that he had everyone's undivided attention before making his final statement. 'You'd better start praying, folks. We're being swept downstream—can't you——'

Before he could say any more Björn's voice came loud and authoritative over the loudspeaker, 'Mr Griffin, will you please return to your seat?'

The salesman paused, then shrugged, and to Alex's relief began his lurching way back. But it was clear his words had caused unrest among the holidaymakers and the murmur of voices grew louder until interrupted again by their driver's reassuring tones.

'Please listen, everyone. What Mr Griffin says is perfectly true, these waters do rise as the day progresses—but you can rest assured that unless I were very, very sure, I would under no circumstances try to cross. We are not, I repeat *not* being swept downstream, and in a few minutes we shall reach the other side with no harm done. This bus is specially built for just such occasions as this, and if you will all remain calm you will find there is nothing at all to worry about. I apologise for Mr Griffin's outburst—no doubt his intentions were good, but it is a case of a little knowledge being dangerous. I sincerely hope, Mr Griffin, that you will not repeat your performance, or I shall have no alternative but to ask you to leave the party.'

Harry's face was even redder by the time Björn

had finished, and it was clear to all that he had taken the point. Let's hope we have no more trouble in his direction, thought Alex. He could be a very nasty character to deal with.

'Now, Alexandra,' Björn turned and spoke quietly, 'please make sure everyone's all right, particularly the women.'

Alex smiled weakly. Now that the moment of tension was over the pain in her ankle was beginning to make itself felt, but she was determined not to complain. Björn had enough to cope with. Gingerly she put her foot to the floor. The pain was unbearable. Stealing a glance at Björn, she saw that all his concentration was on the crossing, and, grateful that he could not see her discomfort, she limped along the gangway, addressing each passenger in turn, giving a word of reassurance where it was needed and relieved to find that everyone had accepted Björn's word in preference to Harry Griffin's.

Austin was the only person to notice anything wrong, for Alex kept a fixed smile on her lips despite the agonies she was experiencing.

'What's the matter?' He touched her cheek lightly. 'You look very pale. Surely you haven't let that idiot upset you?'

Alex shook her head. 'It's nothing, I twisted my ankle. It'll be better in a minute.'

She moved to the next passenger before he could say more, thankful when her task was finished and she could return to her seat.

'Everything okay?' asked Björn, and without waiting for her answer, 'we're almost across now. We'll stop for a few minutes. Let everyone get out and stretch their legs and find out for themselves what a fool that man Griffin is. Why is it that on every journey you get someone like him?'

Alex was hardly listening. Her ankle had begun to swell alarmingly and she felt queasy. She hoped Björn wouldn't notice; she could imagine his irritation once he found out. An invalid courier was all he needed!

After the coach had stopped and the passengers alighted it was impossible for Alex to remain behind without arousing suspicion. Painfully she climbed out, gratefully accepting Austin's arm as she touched the ground. Moss-covered mounds of lava made it slippery underfoot, but she managed to walk the short distance to the rest of the passengers without limping too badly. The Markarfljót was still rising and many fingers were pointed towards the fast stretch of broken water in the middle. Alex could almost hear them thinking what a close shave they had had, but she herself had never doubted for one minute that they would safely ford the swiftly flowing waters. Her faith in Björn was unshakable, and she only wished he had as much faith in her.

'You need that ankle bandaged,' Austin observed as she winced with each step she took. 'Where's your first aid kit? I'll do it for you.'

Alex frowned. 'I suppose we have one somewhere, though I don't remember seeing it.'

'Never mind, my hankie will do,' and before she could protest he had dipped it into the river. 'Sit down.'

With no choice but to agree, Alex awkwardly lowered herself on to the gravelly slope. Austin eased off her shoe and though his touch was gentle Alex murmured in pain, closing her eyes as if to try and shut out the hurt. Then all at once, even before he spoke, she became aware of Björn's presence.

'What the devil's going on?' he demanded in his most imperious voice.

She looked up at the tall strength of him towering above her, into the cold, hard eyes that she had once thought were the most beautiful eyes she had ever seen. There was nothing attractive about them now. Like chips of granite they bored into her soul. She flinched involuntarily. How this man could hurt when he tried.

Austin answered. 'Alex has hurt her ankle. I'm bandaging it for her.'

'So I see,' the voice heavy with impatience. 'How did this happen, Alexandra, and why wasn't I informed?'

'I—I—er—tripped.' She was loth to get Harry into further trouble, but it seemed that Austin had no such qualms.

'It was that fellow Griffin, he pushed her. He ought to be made to apologise.'

'We'll get round to that later. What I want to know now is, why wasn't I told?' Björn squatted beside Alex, resting his arms on his knees. On a level with her he did not seem so forbidding, and she looked steadily back.

'You had enough trouble without me adding to it. It's not much. It will be fine tomorrow.'

Expertly he touched the swollen joint, his thick brows rising expressively. 'I think not. It will take two or three days at least to get over this.' His lips tightened and Alex guessed that he regretted ever asking her to help out on this trip.

'I—I'm sorry, Björn. I'll try not to let it hamper me.' Her eyes were troubled.

'Oh, it's not your fault, it couldn't be helped. It's just damned annoying, that's all—and another thing, why the handkerchief when there's a first aid kit available?'

'I couldn't remember seeing it,' admitted Alex, 'so this seemed the next best thing.'

Björn's eyes narrowed. Suddenly he rose and walked swiftly towards the bus. He was back within seconds—empty-handed, noted Alex in rising alarm. It had been her job to check that everything had been packed. Surely she couldn't have missed anything? She went hot and then cold, and her heart raced uncomfortably. She steeled herself for the expected tirade, not daring to look at him.

But when he spoke she was pleasantly surprised. 'It's my fault,' he said. 'I remember now. I have two kits, one for the bus and one for the kitchen, and I put them both in the kitchen intending to transfer one later. It's a good job nothing more serious happened. Once we reach the valley I'll get it and bandage your ankle properly.'

And now he was actually smiling, Alex felt suddenly joyful. For a space her ankle was forgotten and she smiled back into the smoke-grey eyes. Nothing was as bad as it seemed when he looked at her like that. But her pleasure was shortlived. Juliet's voice, sweetly demanding, called out to Björn. With a murmured, 'Excuse me,' he had gone.

Marvelling at the swiftness of his response, Alex turned her attention to a clump of arctic fireweed growing nearby. She drew strength from the beauty of the unusual purple flowers which grew densely all along the river bank. It was stupid to be so easily hurt, but it was something over which she had no control.

Austin finished tying the handkerchief and helped her to her feet. Although the ankle was still painful, the supporting bandage did help and she was able to hobble back to the bus. He sat beside her and they chatted desultorily until Björn decided it was time to make a move.

Their route took them past the spot where the glacier Eyjafjallajökull descends right down into a lake, a sight which drew many cries of wonder, then through into the valley covered in parts by lush grass and low trees. Had it not been for the wild mountains and glaciers surrounding the valley it could well have been rural England. Most parts of the island were treeless and barren, so that in consequence Thórsmörk appeared more inviting. Here, in this magnificent, awe-inspiring setting, they set up camp for the night.

The first thing Björn did was to fetch the first aid kit from the kitchen truck, which already had a meal waiting for the hungry holidaymakers, and proceed to expertly re-bandage Alex's ankle.

His touch, though light and impersonal, set Alex's

pulses racing, but he frowned as he worked and she could not help but realise what a liability she had become. Tentatively she tried to apologise. 'I—I'm sorry, Björn. I wish——'

'For heaven's sake,' he rasped, 'don't keep on! Perhaps another time you'll know better than to try and appeal to a man of Griffin's type.'

I only did it for you, Alex wanted to say, to save you any trouble. Instead of helping, though, she had made matters worse. She felt near to tears but blinked them back, knowing Björn would not condone a crying woman. 'It feels much better now, thank you. I should be able to walk over to the kitchen truck without any help.'

'Oh no,' he said, 'that's asking for trouble. You're to rest as much as you can for a day or two. I'll manage.' And with that he swung her up into his arms as easily as if she were a child. She could feel the powerful beat of his heart against her side and smell the faint musky odour of aftershave. Her thoughts ran riot for one glorious moment; if she closed her eyes she could imagine that he was carrying her over the threshold, that this was the beginning of their new life together.

Stark reality, in the form of Maggie's broad Scots voice, dragged her back to reality. 'Now what's the young lassie been doing? Bring her in here, Herra Einarsson. I'll look after her.'

'There's no need to fuss, Maggie,' smiled Alex. 'I'm not quite an invalid.'

'Make sure she doesn't try to walk,' instructed Björn. 'She's to rest that ankle as much as possible.

I'll carry her wherever she wants to go.'

Alex flushed, but decided that silence was the best policy. There were some places where he just couldn't take her!

Through the window of the truck she noticed that he was once again at Juliet's side, and she felt suddenly deflated. It was obvious where his interest lay and he was going to find it something of a bore to transport Alex herself continually from one place to another. Austin, passing the window, gave her a sudden idea. She tapped the glass and beckoned him in.

'Do me a favour,' she said at once, 'try and find a branch that will serve as a walking-stick. Then I can get about without being a nuisance to anyone.'

'I'm sure you're never that,' he smiled, 'but if that's what madam wants then madam shall have it,' and giving her a mock bow he disappeared into the nearby birch trees.

Why can't I love *him*? thought Alex, why did I have to fall for someone as impossible as Björn? Austin was kind and considerate, everything she had ever desired in a man; whereas Björn represented the iron master from whom she was trying to escape. Björn was like Gerard, and her grandfather too, both of the same mind and both trying to inflict their wills on her. Why couldn't he be like Austin and treat her as an equal?

As the holidaymakers came to the truck for their meal they all had a sympathetic word for Alex, even Harry Griffin. She had seen Björn talking to him earlier and from his hangdog expression afterwards it looked as though he had fully repented his folly.

Austin returned with a stout stick, the head of which he had carved to form a smooth handle, and after she had finished her meal Alex decided to try it out.

She developed a kind of hopping walk, using the stick in place of her injured leg, and felt quite pleased with her progress. All would have been well had she not caught her good foot on an uneven patch of ground. Momentarily caught off balance, she went sprawling—right at the feet of Juliet and Björn.

Her face red with humiliation, Alex tried to avoid the two pairs of eyes, but it was impossible not to hear the other woman's affected laugh and her pretence of amusement.

'Oh, look, Björn—she's fallen again. Don't you think you ought to get someone a little more stable for your courier?'

But Björn was helping Alex to her feet, and he ignored Juliet's comments. 'Will you never learn?' he said impatiently. 'God knows what we'd have done if you'd hurt your other leg as well. Where do you want to go?'

'Into the coach,' said Alex on the spur of the moment, 'my bag's there and I want to repair my make-up.'

'Surely you could have asked someone to fetch it, instead of trying this tomfool game? What are you trying to prove?'

He lifted her up before she had time to protest, and as he walked towards the bus Alex caught the malevolent look Juliet flashed in her direction. She pretended not to notice, but it hurt to think that anyone hated her enough to react like that. Juliet need not worry; Björn had made it evident often enough that he considered Alex nothing more than a nuisance to be endured only for the period of the tour.

'I'm not trying to prove anything,' her voice sounded thin, unlike her usual confident tones. 'I—I didn't want to be any more trouble.'

He looked down, his face only inches from her own, and his eyes softened fractionally. 'Then I suggest you do as I say.' He mounted the steps and put her gently on to the seat. 'That's an order, understand?' but his voice was so quiet, so kind, that Alex thought she had misheard. He couldn't be speaking to her like that, as though he cared. It was ridiculous.

Almost imperceptibly she nodded, and satisfied now that she would do as he asked, Björn left. Twisting her head, Alex watched him cross the grass as if trying to remember every detail of this beloved man. Not that it was necessary. Stored in her mind were mental pictures of Björn laughing or sad, cross or happy. His relaxed walk, with his thumbs tucked into his hip pockets as they were now, or his stiff and bristling attitude when he was angry. And every line of his strong, square face, the full sensuous lips and the handsome eyes, so thickly fringed that at times it was impossible to see into them clearly: all these were imprinted permanently in her mind.

Instead of returning to Juliet as Alex had expected, he moved into the low woodland and was soon lost to view. Juliet herself must have anticipated he would rejoin her, for she had half-risen when he left the coach. Now she stood staring after him and Alex wondered whether she would follow. Instead she swung round and headed towards the stationary bus and Alex, her beautiful face distorted by anger.

CHAPTER FOUR

JULIET began her attack immediately she reached the bus. 'If you think you're going to attract Björn away from me with your helpless-little-girl tactics,' she hissed, 'you're very much mistaken. It won't work. You're not his type.'

Although Alex had prepared herself she had not expected to see quite so much hatred on the other girl's face. Juliet's nostrils flared, and the once-beautiful lips were drawn into a contemptuous sneer. Her eyes had hardened until they were like twin points of steel and her voice grated harshly.

'I'm sure I don't know what you're talking about.' Alex endeavoured to keep her voice steady, not wishing to let the other girl know how much her words hurt. 'I don't want Björn,' she lied, 'and I'm perfectly sure he has no interest in me.'

Juliet moved forward until she was standing directly in front of Alex. 'That's not the way it looks.

Ever since this trip started you've done nothing but try to keep him away from me. Don't think I haven't noticed. But you won't win—I'll see to that!'

There was positive loathing on her face and Alex shook her head, completely bemused by this unwarranted criticism. 'You've got it wrong.' It was difficult to keep her voice calm. 'Björn employed me to do a job, there's no more to it than that.'

'And a fine mess you're making of it,' taunted Juliet, looking pointedly at the bandaged ankle. 'You don't really expect me to believe that you took this job for the money? I'm no fool, nor is Björn.' She tossed her blonde curls haughtily. 'I guess you had your sights set on our handsome Mr Einarsson and decided this job was the only way you could get him to take notice of you. Let's face it, he wouldn't give you a second glance otherwise.'

At that moment Alex wished with all her heart that she was a man in order that she might forcibly settle this argument; instead she was obliged to restrain herself, and behave in the manner expected of a young lady brought up by the strict Charles Constantine. 'Miss Devale,' she said, 'I don't wish to listen to any more of your insinuations. If you stopped to work this thing out rationally you'd soon realise that there's nothing between Björn and myself—nor ever likely to be. Now will you please leave—my ankle hurts and I want to rest.'

'I bet you do!' Accusing eyes stared at Alex for one long second before their owner moved towards the open doorway. 'I'll go now, but you can rest assured you haven't heard the last of this—unless you take my advice and leave Björn Einarsson alone.'

Never in all her life had Alex felt so passionately angry—yet there was nothing she could do about it. She dared not let Björn discover the friction between Juliet and herself, for he would most certainly want to know the reason, and no doubt Juliet would dream up some perfectly logical excuse, blackening Alex's character even further into the bargain.

Repeatedly she clenched her fists, wishing there was something she could do. She felt so inadequate. 'Oh, darn Harry Griffin!' she cried aloud. 'If I hadn't hurt my ankle none of this would have happened.'

'Talking to yourself?' Austin's smiling face appeared round the door and looked inquiringly in her direction.

But even Austin's presence wasn't welcome in her present frame of mind, and Alex scowled blackly. 'What does it look like?'

His eyes widened. 'Gosh, who's upset you?'

Alex had to smile at his concern. 'I'm sorry. Come in and I'll tell you all about it.' If she didn't share her unhappiness with someone she would burst, and Austin was the only person she felt could be trusted.

He watched her warily as he climbed the steps, pretending to be afraid, edging along until he reached her seat and then sitting on the edge furthest away.

In the end Alex burst into laughter. 'Oh, Austin, you are an idiot! I won't bite, at least not you.'

'Come on, then,' he said, relaxing back into the

seat, 'out with it. Although I think I can guess who the culprit is—our beautiful Juliet, am I right?'

Alex nodded. 'Do you know I nearly hit her? Me—who's never had a harsh thought about anyone in my life. If she hadn't gone when she did I'd be out of a job right now.'

'So you almost had a fight.' The corners of his mouth pulled down wryly. 'She must have said something pretty nasty for you to feel like that.'

'Too true. She accused me of trying to steal Björn away from her. Have you ever heard anything so ridiculous? You know better than anyone how he treats me.' She found it surprisingly easy to talk like this without giving away the true state of her feelings regarding Björn. She presumed that her annoyance with Juliet had the effect of overriding her real emotions.

'She's jealous because she's not getting all her own way.' Austin's tawny eyes were amused. 'I shouldn't let her bother you, women of her type aren't worth it.'

'But I can't help worrying,' insisted Alex. 'The way she acted, I shall be on edge every time I speak to Björn. I can just imagine her taking great pleasure in dragging those red talons of hers down my cheeks.'

'You're letting your imagination run riot,' said Austin, pulling her hands into his to try and stop their restive twisting. 'I don't think she'd really go so far as that. But if it will make you feel any better I have a suggestion to make.'

Alex looked at him questioningly. 'If it will stop

Juliet digging her claws in, I'm all for it.'

'Wait until you've heard what I have to say,' he warned, 'you may not like the idea.' He paused, allowing her time to compose herself before he said, 'You do like me, don't you, Alex?'

'But of course,' she laughed, 'though I don't see what that's got to do with——'

'Hang on,' he broke in, 'give me chance to finish. I don't quite know how to put this, but if you and I—er—developed a closer relationship, I think that should effectively quieten our pretty friend.'

'You mean——?' Alex knew what he meant, it was just that she needed time to think about it. She liked Austin a lot—but not in that way, though it would solve her problem. And what did he think about her? Was he serious? Did he see this as a way of speeding up their relationship, or was he acting purely out of kindness? There was Björn to be considered too. He had already reprimanded her for being too friendly with this man—what would *his* reaction be? She was torn between two evils.

Austin wisely remained silent, giving her time to weigh up the matter and reach a decision. In the end she decided to agree to Austin's idea, for Björn's wrath would be easier to bear than Juliet's accusations, which would condemn her even more in her employer's eyes than a holiday romance with Austin. 'Though there can never really be anything between us,' she added quickly.

'There's someone else?' He swiftly hid the disappointment that shadowed his eyes, but Alex observed it and wondered whether she was doing the right thing. If he was attracted to her, was there any point in allowing him the luxury of a romance which would finish as soon as the tour ended? It seemed hardly fair to accept in these circumstances. Sensing her hesitation Austin smiled. 'I see I'm right, but I'd still like to help if you'll let me?'

'Very well,' but feeling she owed him an explanation, Alex continued, 'the man I love—well, he doesn't know, but I feel I ought to——'

'You don't have to explain,' he put a finger gently on her lips, 'but I appreciate it all the same. Now we both know where we stand we can get down to the serious business of becoming—er—lovers.' There was a twinkle in his eye as he spoke and Alex felt reassured, relieved.

The next moment his lips brushed hers and she drew back in protest. This was something she hadn't bargained for. 'Austin! What do you think you're doing?'

'Sealing our bargain,' he smiled, and putting one hand behind her head he guided her gently so that his lips were once again on hers. There was no passion in his caress; as he had said, it was merely a token of friendship, but Alex was aware of the strict control he held over his own emotions and withdrew as soon as she could without hurting his feelings. He was too nice to hurt. Dear, kind Austin! Again she wondered why she couldn't have fallen for him.

'A pity about your ankle,' he said, 'or we could have gone for a walk. It's so pleasant here.' He looked ruefully through the window as he spoke at the dazzling snow-capped mountains and the towering rocks just asking to be climbed, and Alex knew he was longing to be out there, exploring, instead of cooped up here inside the coach.

'Please don't stay here on my behalf, I've seen it all before. This is your holiday. You must make the most of it.'

'If you're sure——?' He rose, but still hesitated.

Alex gave him a push. 'Of course I am, now go before it's too late.'

Left alone with her thoughts, Alex contemplated the wisdom of their arrangement. Although it would please Juliet to think that Alex had fallen for Austin, Björn was going to be angry—more explosive than ever before. It would help, though, for under his wrath she would be able to forget her own feelings. It might even cure her, for what future was there in loving him? He had made it clear that he considered her spoilt. Her height did not help, nor the fact that she had never worked before. She could imagine the mental picture he must have of a sweet, innocent child brought up under the protective wing of an ageing grandfather, with no more idea of the ways of the world than if she had spent her childhood in an orphanage.

I can assure you, Herra Einarsson, she said crossly to herself, that I'm well able to take care of myself—whatever you may think!

She closed her eyes and must have slept, for the next thing she knew was being woken by Mrs Shaw gently shaking her shoulder. 'Mr Einarsson sent me to see if you were awake. I said it was a shame to disturb you, but he said you can't stay here all night.'

Her concern touched Alex and she smiled. 'What time is it? I didn't intend to go to sleep.'

'Almost ten. The tents are all ready, and Mr Einarsson said that if you need any help he'll be only too willing——'

'I can manage perfectly well,' began Alex hastily, stopping when she saw Mrs Shaw's surprised expression. 'I mean, it's very kind of him to offer, of course, but after all, it's only my ankle.'

'Such a horrid man, that Mr Griffin,' continued Mrs Shaw, 'he quite spoilt my day yesterday and I was so enjoying it. I saw what he did to you, and I said to Mr Shaw, the younger generation have no manners at all. I don't know what the world's coming to.'

'I'm sure it was an accident,' replied Alex, 'he didn't meant to hurt me. I'm pleased to hear you're enjoying your holiday. Have you been abroad before?'

Mrs Shaw shook her head. 'Never. We've always gone to Bournemouth. I had such a job persuading Joe, but as I said, we'll never be able to afford it again, so eventually he agreed. It's a wonderful country. It's all so different, and not only the scenery. I've never seen so many black sheep or brindle cows. I shall certainly have something to tell my grandchildren when we get back.' Her eyes were bright, and there was an eagerness about her face that made Alex feel happy that they had at least one satisfied customer.

Alex had hoped that her ankle might feel easier the next morning, but after several hours' rest it had stiffened considerably and was even more uncomfortable. With the aid of her stick she managed to make her way slowly to the nearest river where she washed in the crystal clear waters. On the way back she met Austin.

'And how's my girl this fine sunny morning?' he greeted her.

Alex smiled and then grimaced as she put her foot to the floor, forgetting for a second the offending ankle. 'I'd be all right if it wasn't for this silly leg,' she said. 'It's pretty painful today.'

'Rest here a while,' he said, indicating a grassy mound. 'As soon as I've washed I'll help you back. You ought to have had more sense than to try it alone.'

Alex pulled a face. 'You sound like Björn when you talk like that, but I'll be glad to sit down all the same.'

It was pleasant, relaxing in the shadow of the trees, with the early morning sun filtering through the branches of the birch and willow, dappling the grass in beautiful intricate patterns, and listening to the chatter of the birds. Due to Thórsmörk's sheltered position it was warmer here than in the neighbouring areas, and Alex felt comforted and at peace with herself. Although the lack of trees in other parts of Iceland resulted in unobstructed views and the rugged grandeur of the island could be fully appreciated, she preferred these fertile valleys where the grass grew greener and shrub and woodland enhanced nature's beauty.

When Austin returned she was loth to leave her peaceful spot, but realising she couldn't stay there for ever she reluctantly allowed him to help her up.

'You look as though you want to stay,' Austin smiled gently, his hand still holding hers even though she was now standing.

Strangely enough Alex did not mind. 'I feel happier here than I have since we started. It's so serene—I feel that all at once my cares have been soothed away.'

He kissed the tip of her nose. 'I can feel it too, but I don't know about you, I'm ready for my breakfast.'

Alex nodded. 'I am a bit hungry.' And so, with her stick in one hand and Austin's ready arm taking her weight on the other side, she managed to hop along quite easily.

They had neared the clearing where the tents were pitched when Björn appeared. Alex was laughing at some remark of Austin's, her face unusually animated as she looked up at her companion, but she stopped short when she saw her employer, for he looked anything but pleased. His brows were drawn together as they so often were of late, and his lips were set in a grim, straight line. But if she were going to pretend an affair with Austin she would have to learn to accept this, decided Alex, and she might as well start now. So, pretending not to notice his displeasure, she called out a bright 'Good morning.'

He ignored her greeting. 'Do you think it fair to take up the time of one of our visitors? If you'd only waited I was quite prepared to help.'

'I don't mind,' Austin spoke before Alex could answer, 'besides, I offered. I couldn't see a lady hobbling along with a stick—especially someone so pretty as Alex.' He shot her an admiring glance and his grip on her waist tightened.

Alex's cheeks flamed. Wasn't it Juliet they were out to convince, not Björn? Nevertheless she smiled up at the Englishman. 'You're very gallant. I'm sure I'd never have managed without your help.'

'This is truly a beautiful spot,' continued Austin. 'I must congratulate you, Mr Einarsson, on your country. It's rightly called a land of contrasts. Where else would you find hot springs and glaciers one minute and green, fertile valleys the next?'

Looking slightly mollified, Björn replied, 'I'm glad you like it, but you've seen nothing yet. Wait until you've experienced bathing in the hot springs, visited the lunar-like landscape of the interior and travelled up part of the mighty Vatnajökull by special snowcat. Then you'll truly have something to talk about. Let's hope your ankle mends quickly, Alexandra, for I'm sure our friend here doesn't want to be hampered by you all the time, no matter how *gallant* you say he is.'

'It's no trouble, I assure you,' said Austin. 'Alex and I have become—er—good friends, and what's a friend for if he can't help out?'

Björn inclined his head. 'Very commendable, but as I understand you're a geologist I should think you'd want to spend your time more profitably. Iceland is a geologist's paradise and I should hate to think you were passing up any opportunities because of my'—he looked down at Alex, and paused a moment before continuing—'my clumsy little courier.'

'That's not fair!' she returned hotly before giving herself time to think. 'It was Harry Griffin's fault, and well you know it.'

'He reckons he hardly touched you,' drawled Björn, 'but that's neither here nor there. The damage is done, and I have to put up with it whether I like it or not.'

Anyone would think *he* had the twisted ankle, thought Alex angrily. But he needn't worry, she would show him that it did not stop her from carrying out her job just as efficiently. 'I'll try not to let it hinder me,' she said drily, and then smiling at Austin, 'if you wouldn't mind helping me just once more?'

Awareness of Björn's disapproving gaze made Alex cling more tightly to Austin than was necessary. Not that Austin minded, he seemed to be enjoying the situation.

He insisted on pulling her tent down himself and waiting on her at breakfast, and when Alex saw the satisfied look on Juliet's face she knew that their plan was working. The trouble was it also had the effect of Juliet paying more attention to Björn, which only made Alex feel worse. She had guessed this would happen, but to see them together like this, with Björn clearly enjoying the blonde's company, was like turning a knife in her heart. Consequently she was more friendly with Austin than she had intended.

'Where are we heading today?' he asked, when they had almost finished breakfast.

'Our first stop is the waterfall Skógarfoss,' she replied. 'We shall have lunch there and then carry on to Vik, which is a little trading centre, and then along the "Back of the Mountains" track to the Fire Gorge—or Eldjá, to give it its proper name.'

'Ah, yes, I've read about Eldjá—a volcanic chasm about twenty miles long, if I remember rightly—one of Iceland's most interesting sights, splitting mountains and valleys on its course.'

Alex laughed. 'I can see you don't need a courier to tell you what Iceland's all about.'

'But I need a girl to keep me company.' He stopped drinking his coffee and looked intently at Alex.

If I'm not careful, she thought, I can see myself heading into danger, even though he knows that my heart belongs elsewhere. I really mustn't encourage him.

'You flatter me,' she said, trying to dismiss his lightly-spoken words. 'Don't forget ours is a friendship of convenience. I'm very grateful to you for trying to help get Juliet off my back, but I don't want you to forget that it can never be anything more.'

He smiled ruefully. 'You won't let me forget. But

never fear, I'll not be a nuisance, except that I may not be able to help myself. You see, dear Alex,' he paused, twisting his cup round and round, 'I love you. I wasn't going to tell you, but I can't help it. You're so lovely and—and so—what can I say? You're like a fragile porcelain and I feel I want to protect you for the rest of your life.'

For a moment Alex could only sit and stare. She had suspected he was attracted—but not this. It now made his plan impossible. How could she ask for his friendship, his help? It was unfair. It would be like kindling the love of a puppy and then turning it out into the cold when you found you didn't want it. She couldn't do this to Austin.

'I—I wish you hadn't said that.' Her green eyes were worried and a tiny frown creased her brow.

'Why? It won't make any difference. I already knew how I felt before I offered to help you out.' Then his voice saddened. 'It will be better than nothing.'

Alex laid a hand on his arm. 'That's just it. Don't you see, Austin, I can't do it to you. If I hadn't known how you felt, it wouldn't have mattered; it was a game, but now—well, you know what I mean.' She bowed her head, unable to go on.

'Austin said firmly, 'Look at me, Alex,' and as she slowly raised her eyes, 'I know what I'm taking on and I don't ask for anything more. Maybe a kiss or two for the sake of Juliet, but I don't want you to distress yourself on my behalf. We men are built of sterner stuff than you women, and I'm prepared to accept gratefully what life has to offer without feeling sorry for myself when it doesn't turn out the way I want it. There'll be no tears, no regrets.' He touched her cheek with his forefinger, tracing the soft curve, and then cupping her chin in his hand he leaned forward and gently kissed her.

Alex closed her eyes against the tears that threatend, and when she looked at him again it was through a misty blur that she saw his brown eyes regarding her tenderly, his lips curved into a smile, and she knew that in Austin she had found a rare kind of friendship. And because she didn't want to hurt him any more than was necessary she told herself that in time, if she tried very hard, she might be able to return his love. 'You're so kind,' she said at last. 'I wish things were different.'

'If we all had our wishes granted the world would be a pretty uninteresting sort of place,' he returned. Grab what you can when you can, that's my motto. Life's too short to do otherwise.'

It was not until they were on their way to Skógarfoss that Björn indicated that he had seen Austin kiss her. The passengers were talking between themselves; now that they had got to know one another there existed an amity between them which had been non-existent in the beginning. Even Harry Griffin seemed to have settled down, forgetting his previous knowledge of the island and discussing the day's arrangements with interest. At the onset of the journey Alex had told them what to expect and where they would be stopping, and now they seemed perfectly content to chat together.

In her own seat Alex avoided looking at Björn,

instead turning her head to watch through the window. There was always something different to be seen, even though she had travelled this road many times in the past. Her grandfather had always driven on these occasions, hiring a Landrover for the journey, which Alex had thought incongruous when associated with Charles, although it was one of the best forms of transport, as many roads were little more than dirt tracks. Only the large towns such as Reykjavik and Akureyri boast asphalt roads, while the other main ones have gravel surfaces which tend to form potholes when the weather is wet.

She sensed rather than saw Björn look at her. 'You're playing a dangerous game,' he said, his voice low so that he would not be overheard.

'I beg your pardon?' Alex turned her head and frowned, pretending not to understand.

He was once again scanning the road, his back straight and his head proudly erect even while driving. Alex tried to shut out the fact that she loved every inch of this man, from the black, wiry hair curling into the nape of his neck down to the tip of his Icelandic boots.

'I see you've taken little notice of my warning not to get too friendly with Austin Maddison,' he said curtly. 'There's nothing more I can do, but I think you're being very foolish.'

Once again Alex felt her anger rising. Why did he always have to pick on her? Couldn't he find it in his heart to say something nice for once? 'I have a right to choose my own friends. I'm sorry you don't approve, but I find Austin a most charming and considerate companion. Of course,' she was unable to resist adding, 'I shall see that my friendship doesn't affect my job.'

'I shall be watching that too,' returned Björn. 'You can rest assured you'll be under constant observation. Holiday romances rarely last, so if you want my advice you'll play it cool or you might find yourself let down with a bang.'

Alex smiled to herself. If only he knew! 'I'll be careful. I'm not the innocent you think.'

'We're not discussing your virtues, Alexandra. You've had a sheltered upbringing, and to a certain extent I feel responsible for you. Jón told me the type of man your grandfather was.'

I bet you don't know that you're the same, thought Alex unkindly. But what she said was, 'I'm grateful that you should feel so concerned, but I assure you you have no need to worry. I know exactly what I'm doing.'

He left it at that, and began discussing the day's programme. 'And I'm glad to see everyone's settling down at last,' he concluded, 'even our friend Griffin. I must admit I had my doubts, but I think he'll be all right now.'

Looking back along the length of the bus Alex said, 'I think he's enjoying himself. The others seem to have accepted him now, and he's airing his knowledge without being too ostentatious.'

'Perhaps it will ease your load until your ankle's better.' In one of his sudden changes of temperament Björn's voice had softened. 'How is it today? Still painful?'

And ridiculously, Alex found herself responding. She despised her reaction, but supposed it was one of the hazards of falling in love. 'It's not too bad,' she admitted, 'although it was very stiff first thing.'

'I'll re-dress it when we get to the waterfall,' he said. 'I should really have done it first thing.'

'Please don't bother. I can do it myself,' but deep down Alex hoped he would insist, even though his touch would be sweet torture. With every hour that passed, every minute spent in the company of this disturbing man she longed for physical contact, even if only in the form of a clinical detachment as he bound her ankle.

'It's no trouble at all,' he was saying. 'While our party are admiring the thunderous Skógarfoss I'll tend to your ankle. You and I have seen it all before, and it doesn't matter if we miss it this time. I don't think we need fear that any one of our members will do anything foolish while we're not there to supervise. What do you say?'

Both surprised and pleased that he should ask her opinion, Alex said, 'I'm sure they'll be all right,' although she could not think why he had asked. After all, it would take but a few minutes to bandage her leg, and then he could join the others. Unless he intended staying behind to keep her company? This seemed such an unlikely proposition that Alex laughed.

He glanced across and smiled too. 'Have I said something funny?' One eyebrow quirked crookedly upwards.

'No, I just thought of something that amused me.'

'Can't we both share the joke?'

'I doubt if you'd see it in the same light. Aren't we almost there?'

As she anticipated, this put a stop to the conversation, but even those few words spoken without aggression made her feel much happier. She smiled confidently to herself as the passengers prepared to leave. It was not until Juliet paused beside them and asked Björn whether he was going with her that her feeling of well-being was disrupted.

'Not this morning, I'm afraid,' he said. 'I must see to Alexandra's ankle.'

Whether he saw the malicious look she gave Alex, Alex herself did not know; she was only aware that her pleasure had been spoiled and that Juliet must now be thinking she had deliberately asked Björn to tend her ankle. So much for her arrangement with Austin! It didn't look as though it would work after all.

The bus emptied, leaving Alex and Björn alone. She looked expectantly across, assuming he would immediately see to her leg, but instead he pulled out his cigarettes and smoked in silence for a few minutes, lazily watching a fly as it crawled across the windscreen.

Through the window Alex saw Juliet talking to Austin. She laughed provocatively up into his face and then tucking her arm through his they followed the rest of the party. She looked over her shoulder at the bus as they went, and Alex knew that she had done this deliberately and was checking to make sure she had been seen.

'I shouldn't worry too much about those two,' Björn said, 'Juliet is the type who will attach herself to any man if she feels neglected.'

Alex had not realised that Björn was also watching and turned now, surprise on her face. 'Why should I worry? Austin's perfectly free to choose whatever friends he likes.'

'You rather gave the impression that he meant more to you than that—or was I mistaken?' His eyes narrowed through the thin screen of smoke, and Alex knew he was deliberately leading her on.

She shrugged. 'I like him, yes, but there's no more to it than that. He's been very kind to me this last couple of days, and I appreciate it.'

'How about the boy-friend back home? What's he going to say when he finds out?'

Alex shot him an indignant look. 'Don't you ever listen to me? I've already told you twice that I have no boy-friend.'

He held up a finger. 'Correction, you said you had fallen out with him. There's a subtle difference. Quarrels can always be patched up.'

'This one won't,' she stated.

'You sound very sure. Would you care to tell me about it—or is it too personal?' He smiled—an insolent smile, decided Alex, as she tossed the question over in her mind. She couldn't quite understand Björn in this mood. In the end she elected to tell him, if only to stop further questions. He seemed in some peculiar way interested in Gerard.

'Gerard didn't want me to come to Iceland. When grandfather died Gerard wanted us to get married, but I felt I wasn't ready to be tied down.'

His eyebrows quirked in the way she was beginning to recognise. 'Is that how you regard the state of matrimony?'

'To Gerard it would have been,' she explained. 'He's like my grandfather, he forgets the march of progress. As far as he's concerned we might as well be living in the last century.'

'How interesting. Do tell me more about this—this Gerard of yours.'

He was mocking her now, but deliberately ignoring the sardonic humour in his eyes, Alex continued, 'There's not a lot to tell. We met when I was seventeen at a party thrown by one of my grandfather's friends. He was different at first, and it wasn't until I got to know him that I found out the way his mind worked. No woman should go out to work, or attend a party unchaperoned, or drink in a pub. I ask you! Have you ever heard anything so ridiculous?'

'I can see Gerard's point of view. In fact I can sympathise with him. There are a few of us left who decry the passing of the age of chivalry.'

Alex glared. 'What has chivalry to do with women doing a job of work? I agree the manners of some young people today leave a lot to be desired, but that's nothing to do with the liberation of women.'

He laughed. 'You're no more than a teenager yourself.'

'I'm twenty-two,' Alex declared huffily, 'but I

don't see what age has to do with it. It's the state of mind that counts.'

'And your Gerard has the mind of his Victorian counterpart?' Björn inquired.

'He isn't *my* Gerard,' retorted Alex. 'Once he found out that I was coming to Iceland irrespective of his wishes he would have nothing further to do with me.'

'And did this sadden you?' His head on one side regarding her speculatively.

'Far from it,' emphatically, 'I shudder to think what life would be like, married to him.'

'He looked thoughtful. 'It's easy to see that you place me in the same category as Gerard, but how about Austin? How does he compare?'

About to deny that Björn was anything like Gerard, Alex realised this wasn't strictly true. Her love had begun to blind her to his faults. When she looked at the facts logically there was little to choose between the two, except that she could never see Gerard branching out into a venture of this sort. He had a very sedate, very secure nine-to-five office job, and would set off at precisely the same time each morning, with furled umbrella and bowler—the typical British city gentleman. She smiled as she remembered how once she had thought him a very suitable marriage partner. He would be reliable, of that there was no doubt, but also very dull; he never did anything unexpected or unpremeditated. Change was an unknown factor in his life, and this was why he had been so horrified when Alex announced her intentions of going to Iceland.

But Björn was waiting for her answer. 'Austin? I hadn't really thought about it, but I suppose he compares very favourably. In fact he's the complete opposite. I've never asked him, but I've no doubt he would agree that we're living in a woman's world.'

'I can't say that you've impressed me with *your* efficiency.' He studied the smoke spiralling from his cigarette, and seemed to be speaking more to himself than Alex. 'It strikes me that you women need to take a much closer look at yourselves.'

'You're insufferably rude,' said Alex hotly. 'I don't see why I should sit here and listen to you any longer.' Forgetting about her ankle, she rose suddenly. It was not until the white-hot pain shot up her leg that she remembered, and subsided limply back on to her seat.

'You silly idiot,' he murmured, but he was beside her instantly with the offending ankle lifted on to the seat. Gently he removed the bandage. 'The swelling's gone down, but you need complete rest, and hobbling about with a stick won't help. For the next two days you're not to go anywhere unless someone carries you—do you hear? By then it should have improved sufficiently for you to use it, in moderation.'

'If you insist.' Alex felt subdued. She always seemed to make a fool of herself in front of him. 'But I hate being a nuisance.'

'You'll be more trouble if you're laid up altogether,' he said impatiently. 'We're not on a picnic.

The worst part of the journey is yet to come.'

He left her then and went over to the kitchen truck, where preparations for lunch were already under way, returning shortly with a basin of water. He bathed the ankle before firmly tying it up again. All the time Alex was aware of his touch, and closed her eyes to try and shut him out.

'I'm not hurting?'

She looked at him then. The grey eyes, dark and concerned, were within inches of her own. Disturbed, Alex shook her head.

But his touch was even more gentle and the pain in her heart infinitely more agonizing. Why do I feel like this, she asked herself, when he's given me no reason to like him? She contented herself with the thought that once the trip was over she would be able to push him from her mind and forget the torments his nearness brought.

The Shaws joined Alex for lunch and she was glad, for Juliet was still clinging determinedly to Austin. Björn had been given the cold shoulder and Alex felt distinctly uneasy. Juliet was trying to stir up more trouble.

It was after lunch that the blonde attacked. Austin had disappeared and the Shaws gone to take photographs near the falls; Alex saw her coming and guessed what was going to happen.

'Mind if I join you?' The honeyed tones did not deceive Alex as the other girl slid down on to the blanket beside her. 'I see Björn made a good job of your ankle. He certainly took his time about it. It's improving, I hope?'

99

Alex eyed her warily. 'It's fairly comfortable, so long as I don't use it.'

'You mean so long as you can get someone to carry you around. Don't think I didn't see Björn bringing you out here.'

'It was his idea,' retorted Alex, 'I could have managed.'

The blue eyes glittered. 'Then why didn't you tell him? Or are you trying to string along both men now? I must say for a plain little creature like you you're not doing too badly.'

It was the first time Alex had been called plain, and she smiled. She might not be a raving beauty, but she could at least claim her fair share of good looks. It might be interesting to see Juliet Devall herself without the thick make-up she always wore, and which looked so out of place on this kind of tour.

'When I saw you with Austin I thought you'd taken heed of my warning,' persisted Juliet. 'You're being very foolish, you know I want Björn.'

'I don't see what that has to do with me,' said Alex levelly. 'I'm sure Björn will make friends with whoever he pleases.'

'There are ways of making a man believe he's doing the chasing.' A complacent smile appeared on Juliet's lips. 'They need a little persuasion, that's all.'

'I've no doubt you're very adept in the art of persuading,' retorted Alex, beginning to feel irritated. 'I'm sure you won't have any trouble in getting your man.'

'But it will make it all the easier if you keep out of

my way, otherwise you might find I'll take Austin off you as well.'

Without waiting for Alex to answer Juliet rose. Her movements, thought Alex, were like those of a tiger, full of grace and strength and meaning. Her claws were out ready to fight, and she wouldn't retract them until she had won.

CHAPTER FIVE

IT was on the way to Vik that Alex saw Harry Griffin making his way towards her, and she held her breath. Whenever she saw this man she expected trouble, even though he had given her no further cause to believe this.

He sat beside her and nodded towards her ankle. 'I've come to apologise. In fact,' he looked shame-faced, 'Vera bullied me into it. She said I ought to be ashamed of myself.'

The thought of little Vera Griffin bullying her husband made Alex smile. 'Please don't worry. It was one of those things.'

'I thought it was just a little sprain that would soon be better, but I can see it's more than that and I'd like to make amends.'

'That's very handsome of you, but I don't really see what you can do.'

'I know this part of the island pretty well. How about letting me take over your job?'

Alex glanced at Björn to see if he had heard, but his eyes were on the road and he gave no indication that he was even aware of Harry's presence. 'There's not much you can do at present,' she answered, 'except give a running commentary on the passing scenery.'

'Then I'll do that,' he said. 'Never fear, I won't let you down—nor say anything likely to upset the passengers.'

She laughed. 'I believe you, and I appreciate your offer, but of course it's not up to me. Mr Einarsson's the boss.'

At the sound of his name Björn looked across. 'Someone talking about me?'

'I'm just trying to tell the little girl,' said Harry, 'that as her incapacity is all my fault I'd like to take over her job for a while. I fancy myself as a guide. Know this part of the coast like the back of my hand. How about giving me a try?'

Björn looked at Alex and then at Harry. 'If Alexandra doesn't mind, it's okay by me. For today anyway. I'd like her to rest as much as possible.'

Harry returned to his seat well pleased, and Alex closed her eyes and relaxed. Her ankle had throbbed during the night, keeping her awake, and now she fell into a light sleep and did not wake until they reached the trading centre of Vík I Mýrdal. She was surprised when she opened her eyes to find the bus empty, with only Austin Maddison to keep her company.

'Why didn't someone wake me?' she demanded.

'Björn said you weren't to be disturbed, so I

volunteered to stay behind. He's gone off with Juliet.'

Alex felt guilty. 'You needn't have done—I'm sure you would find this area interesting.' She looked up at the high rocks surrounding the settlement. 'Beyond those cliffs,' she said, 'is the volcano Katla, and over there lies an area known as Myrdalssandur. It's a desert of black sand where sub-glacial eruptions have caused havoc in the past. All very interesting from a geological point of view.'

'It's you I'm interested in at the moment,' he returned. 'I was very concerned when I saw you asleep. You're not suffering any after-effects?'

'Only from a sleepless night,' she returned wryly.

'Juliet said you ought to see a doctor.' Austin frowned. 'It's not that bad, is it?'

'Juliet's talking rubbish,' snorted Alex. 'She wants me out of the way.'

'I don't think so. She seemed most concerned.'

How clever of her, thought Alex, she knows exactly what she's doing. If I complain about her now, it will look as though I'm the bitchy one. No doubt she's expressed her concern to Björn as well. 'You haven't fallen for that?' she asked bitterly. 'She had another go at me this morning.'

'Perhaps you were a little overwrought——' he began.

Alex interrupted him furiously. 'Don't say she's getting through to you as well!' Juliet's methods were all too clear, and what was more annoying, they were working. Before she knew it both Austin and Björn would be vying for Juliet's attention, while she herself would be left out in the cold. It sickened her to think of it.

He touched her arm. 'Don't be silly. You know I love you. I was going to say that perhaps you interpreted her wrongly. Anyway, let's forget Juliet. I want you to verify one or two things Harry Griffin said.'

'I hope he didn't get his facts wrong,' Alex was startled out of her anger, 'it would be just my luck for something like that to happen.'

'I don't think so. He pointed out the Westmann Islands and mentioned an eruption in 1973. I wondered if you knew anything about it?'

Alex felt relieved. 'Oh yes, it was on Heimaey. I was there at the time with Grandfather.'

Instead of horror, as expressed by most people when they heard of Alex's adventure, Austin looked incredulously pleased. 'You were actually there? This is great. Do tell me about it.'

Alex smiled. 'It happened so suddenly that no one knew the earth had parted until a solid wall of flame appeared in the sky. What surprised me most was the calmness of the townspeople. No one panicked, and we were all evacuated in a remarkably short time.'

'It must have been an incredible sight,' remarked Austin.

'It was. Don't forget Iceland is sitting on an underground inferno, and the Westmann Islands themselves were created by just such an eruption. I felt so sorry for the islanders; their homes were either covered in black ash or set on fire by lava bombs. The devastation was terrible. Yet they always remained cheerful, and talked of the time they would go back and start building again—on top of the lava if necessary.'

They continued to discuss the eruption of Kirkjufell, as it was called by the townspeople, until the rest of the party returned. Juliet, looking very pleased with herself, actually smiled at Alex, though whether this was simply for Björn's benefit Alex could not be sure. It did seem, however, that for the time being Juliet had forgotten her antagonism. I suppose as long as things are going her way, thought Alex, she can afford to be magnanimous— it's when things go wrong that she tries to take her vengenace out on me.

They spent the night in the volcanic chasm Eldgjá, and after a morning spent sightseeing travelled on to Landmannalauger. The fantasia of vividly-coloured mountains in this area drew cries of admiration. Even Alex, who had seen it many times before, wondered at this particular beauty spot, which is said to be one of the richest spots in Iceland as far as variety of colour is concerned. Blues, greens, purples, white, all blending harmoniously together. But it was not the mountains that attracted most attention, it was the natural pools of warm water. Heated from hot springs, they were a popular spot with holidaymakers and it did not take long for most of the group to don their swimsuits and submerge themselves in the steaming waters. They soon forgot their shivers and marvelled at this natural phenomenon that was unlike anything they had ever experienced in Britain.

Soon everyone except the Shaws and Alex were in the water, and Alex could not help noticing the way Juliet flaunted herself in front of Björn. Dressed in a brief white bikini, she made sure he kept at her side, clinging possessively to his arm if he gave any indication of wanting to mingle.

His body was handsomely tanned with not an ounce of superfluous flesh, and Alex's eyes were drawn to him time and time again. Suddenly he called to her, 'Would you like to come in? It might do you good,' and as she hesitated, 'if you can manage to get changed I'll come and fetch——' The rest of his words were drowned as Juliet fell against him, bringing them both down into the water. It looked like an accident, but Alex knew that the other girl had done it deliberately.

She had been undecided whether to join them, but now she felt a sudden desire to show Juliet Devall that she was not going to have everything her own way. Climbing awkwardly back into the coach, she slipped on her fuschia-coloured swimsuit; although of more modest proportions than Juliet's bikini, it revealed every curve of Alex's slim young body, and she knew she had nothing to fear as far as competing with the other girl was concerned.

Björn appeared on the steps as she was adjusting her cap. His dark hair was a mass of tight curls and rivulets of water ran down his face and body. He smiled, even teeth gleaming whitely against the tan. 'Are you ready?'

Although she tried to control her feelings Alex's heart raced and her throat tightened painfully. She nodded, unable to speak.

'You'll enjoy this, I know,' he said, and although Alex knew he was referring to the water she could not help but twist his words to mean that she would enjoy being carried by him.

The actual physical contact of their unclothed bodies was more electrifying than she had imagined, and by the time they reached the pool she felt breathless. He paused before lowering her into the water. 'Sure you're all right?'

Alex swallowed. 'Perfectly.'

'You look—strange.'

She felt strange. Never before had she experienced such strong emotions. It was like a real pain in the region of her heart. She wanted to cling to him, tell him she loved him, desired him. She closed her eyes to shut out his infinitely dear face. It was more than she could bear. It was far, far better when he was angry. Then she could forget her love, she could answer back, whereas now her throat was dry and she knew that if she tried to speak it would be in a hoarse whisper.

And then she was in the water, its warmth caressing her body. Björn's arm was still about her shoulders, until suddenly, rudely, water was splashed into her face and she heard Juliet calling, 'Come on, Björn, I'm waiting!'

He turned away after assuring himself that Alex would be all right, and then was chasing Juliet across to the other side of the pool. Unbidden tears squeezed from between Alex's lids and she was glad of the water to hide her weakness. In no time at all she was surrounded by the rest of the bathers, and was able to forget her misery amid the general hilarity.

When it was time to come out it was Austin who carried her to the bus, Austin who placed the towel round her shivering shoulders and told her to get dressed quickly. She could not help wondering whether he reacted to her as she did to Björn; after all he did love her, though she was sure it was nothing like her love for Björn. Nothing in the whole wide world could match that. How and why it had happened she could not imagine; all she knew was that the exquisite pain of loving had to be endured somehow, and that only deepening her friendship with Austin would help her to bear the pain.

The fact that both she and Austin loved made a sort of bond between them. It helped to know that he would always be there, if only as a foil for Björn.

The wonderful glow from Björn's touch remained long after they had left Landmannalauger, and Alex sat in her seat wrapped up in her euphoria. She missed the strange looks that he slanted towards her, content for the time to revel in these deeper emotions, oblivious of those around her.

Their route the following day led across the wild and desolate terrain of the central highlands. Here amidst the glaciers and the mountains the track became narrower, and to the eye of the inexperienced almost impassable. Alex could tell by the silence that fell over the passengers that they were more than a little apprehensive, and she wasted no time in assuring them that the track was perfectly safe and had been used many, many times before.

A grim kind of beauty was found here in the desert of sand and lava between the largest glacier in Europe, Vatnajökull, and its smaller counterpart, Hofsjökull. They were heading for Jokuldalur valley at the rim of the glacier Tungnafellsjökull, where they planned to camp for the night. From here there would be an expedition to the ice cap of Vatnajö-kull, for those who wanted to go, in a specially built vehicle called a snowcat which, Alex pointed out, was the same type as used by Fuchs' and Hillary's South Pole Expedition.

The glacial river, Kaldakvisi, had to be crossed before reaching their destination, but this time Harry remained silent and the passengers showed no fear. They were becoming accustomed to the adventures this type of holiday had to offer.

Everything now seemed to be going smoothly. Alex's ankle was almost better, though Björn still forbade her to use it, and Juliet had not bothered her again; on the other hand she was frequently to be seen in the company of both Austin and Björn. It occurred to Alex that Juliet was trying to retaliate, but rather than feel annoyed she felt nothing but pity for this girl who did not seem happy unless she had a man in tow. It was still something of a mystery as to why she had come on this trip. Alex noted that she made copious notes of all they did and her camera was always at the ready, but the enigma remained and would probably never be solved.

Gone was the sunshine on the morning of the trip to Vatnajökull; the sky was heavy with the threat of snow. Nevertheless spirits were high, and the members who were going excitedly put on the extra-warm clothing needed for this high altitude, not forgetting sun-glasses, which were absolutely essential in the snowy and glacial regions.

Alex had looked forward to joining the party, and was very disappointed when Björn insisted she remain behind.

'My ankle's better,' she argued, 'why can't I come?'

'Because I need someone back here to look after the remainder of the group. We shall be gone twelve hours, don't forget.'

He was right, of course, but it didn't stop her feeling dispirited. Especially when Juliet, in her brilliant red windcheater trimmed with white fur, looking for all the world as though she was modelling for *Vogue* magazine, clung possessively to his arm.

And he was hers for the rest of the day. Perhaps this was what hurt most. She knew Juliet would not hesitate to take advantage of the long hours spent beside this man, and who knew how Björn would react? He had already shown signs of being strongly attracted towards this pretty blonde girl, and had caused Alex much anguish as they laughed and talked together.

Austin was often off on his geological surveys, and this left Alex alone. Admittedly she was never without company, for they were now like one big happy family, but it wasn't the same, and she couldn't help remembering how Björn had reprimanded her for fraternising with Austin, yet here he was doing exactly the same thing himself. Did it make any difference that he was the boss of the outfit? Seemingly it did, and since his friendship with Juliet he had not frowned so much on Alex's association with Austin, though she could tell he did not like it. He couldn't really rebuke her again, she thought, not without forfeiting his own pleasure, and she was quite sure he was not prepared to do that.

He had left her now, standing disconsolately beside her tent, his attention concentrated on the red-coated figure beside him. She watched as they climbed into the special bus waiting to transfer them to the snowcat, unaware of the sorry figure she looked until suddenly she felt an arm about her shoulders.

Austin's smile was sympathetic. 'Never mind. It's no good overtaxing your ankle.'

She was glad he thought her disappointment was because of the journey. He could not know she would miss Björn, torturing herself with thoughts of what might happen between him and the sophisticated Juliet.

Alex smiled weakly. 'At least I have you to keep me company, but why haven't you gone with them?'

His arm tightened. 'There are methods in my madness. I guessed you'd stay behind, and the prospect of a whole day in your company was certainly more inviting than a trip across a glacier.'

The brown velvet of his eyes deepened as she looked up at him, and she knew he was as emotionally aware of her as she of Björn. This realisation created a bond between them and she nestled more closely into the crook of his arm. The kiss he gave her was swift and light and entirely unprecedented; but to Alex it might have been the most passionate kiss of all time, for when she looked across at the bus she saw Björn was watching them. Her cheeks flamed scarlet. She knew he must think they had done this on purpose, and could only guess at the construction he might put on the scene. He would wish that he had not left them together, believing they would take advantage of the situation to further their friendship. This might be in Austin's mind, but it wasn't what Alex wanted—at this very moment she wished for nothing more than to be alone with her thoughts.

Instead she must stand at Austin's side and act as though nothing untoward had happened. He even failed to notice her heightened colour, or if he did he said nothing, probably thinking that it was the result of his embrace.

At last the bus departed and they were alone. Several couples had remained behind, including the Shaws and surprisingly enough, the Griffins. Alex felt puzzled by this until Harry said that he had made the trip before and felt it advisable to leave room for others who were travelling in Iceland for the first time. This was so in contrast to the brash

Englishman who had begun the holiday with them, that Alex began to wonder what Björn had said to him. He had certainly been a different man since that first outburst, much to everyone's relief.

Although Alex's ankle felt much better she decided it best not to use it too much, and as the others had gone exploring, including Maggie and Erik, the driver of the kitchen truck, only Austin and herself remained at the camp. The weather was now too cool to sit out of doors, so they decided to make use of the tourist hut situated not far from their camp.

All over Iceland similar huts are found for the stranded traveller, or, as was the case with this particular hut, for use by members of the Iceland Tourist Association for weekend outings. As it was early in the season the hut was not yet in use, and Alex and Austin were able to avail themselves of the heating and cooking facilities provided.

The stove soon warmed the little hut and Alex perched on one of the wooden bunks while Austin heated water for coffee.

'You know,' he said, squatting before the stove to warm his hands, 'Juliet's quite a nice person when you get to know her.'

'I'm sure she is,' replied Alex, though there was something in her tone that caused Austin to look up sharply.

'I don't mean I'm falling for her,' he added, 'but I've found her very different from first impressions.'

Alex sniffed. 'Have you forgotten the way she

treated me, how she implied that I was trying to steal Björn away from her?'

'How could I forget,' he laughed, 'when it brought us closer together? I suppose I should be grateful.'

'I've noticed how you show your gratitude,' snapped Alex. 'You seem to find her company more attractive than mine these days.'

He raised his brows. 'Do I detect a little sarcasm, or,' on a lighter note, 'am I beginning to mean something to you after all?'

He rose and crossed to the bunk, his eyes level with her own. He took her face between his hands. 'Am I, Alex?'

She slipped from his embrace and took up the position he had vacated in front of the stove. 'I'm sorry, but I did warn you.' She really did sympathise with this man, for she knew only too well how he felt, how his heart must be torn in two. She wished she could learn to love him; it would be an answer to all her problems. But it was like asking the impossible. One could not change love for convenience's sake.

'This man who you profess to love—why can't you tell him? Is he married or something?'

Alex shook her head. 'Nothing like that. He—he doesn't love me, that's all.'

Austin moved until he could see her face. 'He's told you this?'

'He doesn't have to tell me, I know. He has—another girl-friend.' Or he will have if Juliet gets her way, she finished beneath her breath.

'Then why waste your love where it's not wanted,

114

when there's someone like me ready to step into his shoes?' he demanded.

Alex hesitated. 'You could be right. I wish I knew what to do—oh, quick, the kettle's boiling!'

He made coffee and they sat side by side on the bunk, sipping the warming liquid, each deep in their own personal thoughts.

'Alex,' he said at length, 'you don't have to answer if you don't want to, but—is it Björn?'

Resolutely she kept her eyes fixed on her cup. She was silent for so long that he thought she had not heard, and repeated his question.

Slowly then, she raised her head. Her eyes were troubled as she looked at him and slowly, almost imperceptibly, she nodded.

How it happened she did not know, but the next moment she found herself lying in Austin's arms. His mouth was on hers, passionate, demanding—and she was responding! All the love that belonged to Björn she was giving to him. Unable to resist, she used him as an outlet for her pent-up emotions. In a fervour of excitement she returned his kisses, for in her innermost mind it was Björn she was kissing, Björn whose hands caressed her body, who pressed her close to him until at last, breathless and shaken, he stopped.

It was not until then that Alex realised what she had done, and covered her face with her hands. Tears of humiliation stung her eyes and she was afraid to look at her companion.

She heard his voice, faltering and contrite. 'Alex, look at me.' He pulled her hands away, compelling her to face him. He too looked ashamed, and Alex felt sure there was a suspicion of tears on his lashes as he began his apology. 'How can you ever forgive me? Alex, my dear, I'm so sorry. I don't know what came over me. It was just that seeing your face so troubled, I—I wanted to help.'

His distress was genuine, and Alex reached up and touched his cheek. 'You couldn't help it. I know exactly how you feel.'

'I suppose you do.' He laughed faintly. 'We're both a couple of idiots, giving our love where it's not wanted.'

'Please don't say that. I would like to love you, honestly I would, but I can't help loving Björn, as you can't help loving me. But I do like you, Austin. I like you a lot, and I hope you'll still go on liking me, even though'—she wavered—'even though I can't give you anything more than friendship.'

'So you didn't mean it—when you kissed me?'

She shook her head. 'I'm sorry. It was reaction, that's all.'

He sighed. 'What do we do now? Can you forget what happened?'

'I'll try. I suppose it was stupid coming here. It was bound to happen. We were both so keyed up, but I feel better now—you too, I hope?'

He grinned. 'You're an angel, Alex. It's no wonder I love you. Shall we tidy up and go back?'

Alex was surprised to find it was lunchtime by the time they returned. They had been missed and the smiling glances in their direction told them that the others were putting their own construction on their disappearance. Only Vera and Harry were absent, and as they had all been instructed to return for lunch Alex felt a little apprehensive.

When mid-afternoon arrived and they had still not put in an appearance, she began to feel really worried. In a couple of hours Björn would return, and she could imagine his annoyance if he found that two of their members were missing.

A search was made of the immediate area, but as no one knew which direction they had taken it was a futile effort.

'I shouldn't fret too much,' consoled Austin, 'Harry knows this area, or so he says. He probably hasn't realised the time and will turn up soon wondering what all the fuss is about.'

Realising the logic behind this statement, Alex tried to compose herself, but as time went on she paced restlessly up and down, frequently consulting her watch and with a growing awareness of the pain in her ankle as she refused to sit and rest.

Where were they? Had they no consideration for the others? Didn't Harry know they would all be concerned? Especially Alex herself, who had been left in charge.

At seven the bus returned from the Vatnajökull expedition, and their smiles faded when they saw the faces of the rest of the party. Björn immediately sought out Alex.

'What's the matter?' He spoke in Icelandic, as he always did when he was annoyed or worried. 'Why are you all standing about looking anxious?'

'I'm afraid Vera and Harry are missing,' said Alex,

sticking out her chin and deciding there was nothing to be gained by holding back the information. 'They went out shortly after you'd left and we haven't seen them since.'

His eyes narrowed. 'Did you give them a time limit?'

'One o'clock. Everyone else was here, but not the Griffins. We've searched the area. I—I didn't know what else to do, except wait.'

'They should have told you where they were going. It's your job to know.' He paused a moment before adding suspiciously, 'What were you doing while these people were getting themselves lost?'

Colour flooded her cheeks. 'I—I was with Austin.'

'Hmph!' He fixed his gaze on her flushed face. 'I see. You need say no more. It happened while you were busy—entertaining your young man.'

He was being unfair! It made no difference that she was with Austin; it was an unfortunate coincidence that Björn didn't hesitate to use.

He turned away from her now, and gathered the party round him. 'We'll split into eight groups,' he said, 'and radiate out from this point. Alexandra, you'll remain here in case they return.' He handed her a whistle. 'Give three blasts on this if they do, to let the others know.'

For a while the sound of voices kept Alex company, but very soon they were too far away to hear. A deathly silence took over. An eerie silence. She glanced fearfully over her shoulder at each little sound; the wind whistling through the gullies and an occasional fall of snow on the higher slopes.

Before long the threatened snow began to fall, but she was afraid to take shelter. It was far safer here in the open than huddled in her tent where she could not see what terrors lurked outside. She pulled the hood of her anorak over her head and folded her arms to try and keep out the cold; the temperature had dropped considerably since the onset of the tour, and fear as well as coldness added to Alex's misery.

A sudden noise behind caused her to whirl round in alarm. 'Austin!' she breathed thankfully. 'Am I glad to see someone!'

'I didn't like to think of you here alone,' he said, 'so I doubled back. There's enough of them to cover the area without me.'

During the summer Iceland benefits from perpetual daylight, so Alex was reasonably sure that the Griffins would be found. She said as much to Austin.

He smiled. 'I wish I had your confidence. Björn seemed pretty mad when he found out. I'm sorry he blamed you, I can guess how you felt.'

It was nice to have sympathy, thought Alex, and was glad Austin knew about Björn. Somehow it made her burden easier to bear. She smiled at him.

'I'm beginning to expect trouble whenever I see Björn. It seems I can do no right in his eyes.'

The next moment Harry and his wife came into sight, followed by Valerie and Brian Danks and then Björn. The couple looked very subdued, though none the worse for having spent the last twelve hours away from camp.

'Where'd you find them?' called Austin, ignoring the surprised look Björn gave him.

'Wandering along a little-used track a couple of miles north from here,' he replied grimly. 'They'd lost all sense of direction and were hoping we would send out a search party.'

Harry spoke. 'I'm awfully sorry for the trouble I've caused. I really had no idea we were lost until it was time to return. I thought I knew exactly where I was.'

'Perhaps another time you'll think twice before going off like that,' retorted Björn, 'you were lucky we found you. Pass me the whistle, Alexandra, I'll recall the others.'

While they waited Alex went into the kitchen and heated up soup. They were all wet, besides being tired and cold, but spirits were easily revived and it was not long before everyone was cheerfully discussing Harry and his escapade. Although Alex hoped he had learned his lesson, she could not help but wonder what other trouble this unfortunate man would cause.

When the excitement had died down Björn drew Alex to one side, and she could tell by his expression that it was not a friendly talk he wanted. 'I take a very grave view of this incident,' he began. 'Happily there were no serious consequences, but there could have been, and I want to make sure nothing like it happens again.'

'Surely you're not blaming me for Harry Griffin's stupidity?' She was tired of being the scapegoat every time anything went wrong. It was as though he purposely accused her, and she didn't doubt it was so that he wouldn't ask her to do another tour. He needn't worry—if this was the sort of treatment he doled out she was best away from him. Even her love could not compensate for all this misery.

His voice was cold. 'You were left in charge, and you should have insisted they tell you where they were going. It's easy to get lost along these tracks, but if we had known which direction they had taken our task would have been easier.'

'You know Harry as well as I do,' she retorted, 'he thinks he knows everything. I doubt if he'd have told me if I'd asked.'

'The point is, you didn't. You were too busy elsewhere.'

She glared at him and said nothing.

'This is something else I want to talk to you about. While your ankle was bad I tried to ignore your association with Maddison. He was able to help while I was busy—but now it's better I'd be obliged if you didn't see so much of him.'

'Herra Einarsson,' Alex drew herself up to her full height, 'I may be employed by you, but that doesn't give you the right to choose my friends. If I want to talk to Austin then I shall, and there's nothing you or anyone else can do about it.' She was too annoyed now to care what she said. He had gone too far; he sounded like her grandfather when she had brought home a boy-friend who he considered unsuitable.

His eyes glittered like two chips of ice from the mighty Vatnajökull. 'I have gained the impression, maybe erroneously, that you do rather more than just talk.'

'What are you insinuating?' she demanded furiously. 'That Austin and I are lovers?'

'Something of the kind, though perhaps I wouldn't go that far.'

'You're despicable!' Had they been alone she would have slapped his face. As it was she curled her fingers tightly into her palms and tried to control the white-hot feelings he had aroused. At this moment she hated him.

His eyebrow quirked. 'They say the truth always hurts. I apologise again for being the iron master, but for once you will do as I say.'

'And if I don't?'

'Then I'm afraid you go. There is no room on this trip for love affairs. If the passengers want to amuse themselves then that's up to them, but so far as you or Maggie or Erik is concerned you are here to do a job and I insist you do it properly. That would be impossible if you had your head in the clouds over some young man.'

'I note you don't include yourself in that list,' said Alex drily. 'Are you so different from the rest of us?'

His eyes narrowed. 'What are you getting at?'

'Juliet, who else?' The words were out before she could stop them, but it was true. Why should he get away with it when he was so bitterly opposed to her friendship?

'I see,' he said slowly. 'Jealousy, that explains it.'

He was right. She was envious of the other girl,

but she certainly wouldn't give him the pleasure of knowing. 'Why on earth should I be?' she said scornfully, 'Your affairs are no concern of mine, though I do think you ought to set a good example.' She could tell from the way he frowned that her shaft had struck home and carried on quickly, 'Whenever I look you seem to have Juliet clinging to your arm. Do you think it wise?'

His face whitened beneath the tan. 'You're very impertinent. If we were alone I would take you over my knee and give you a good spanking.'

'I'm only speaking the truth. Does she mean so much to you that you can't bear to be parted?'

'Juliet is alone," he said between clenched teeth. 'She does not make friends easily. I'm merely—being kind to her, as I would anyone in her position. Though why I should excuse myself to you, I don't know.'

'I'll tell you why,' blazed Alex, 'it's so that you won't feel guilty about parting Austin and me. But it won't work—if I want to see Austin I shall. You have no power to rule my life.'

'While you're employed by me I have every right to see that you don't land yourself in trouble. I can't stop you seeing him altogether, I realise that, but I should appreciate it if you would keep your meetings down to a minimum. There are others who might like a little attention.'

She shrugged carelessly. 'I'll bear in mind what you say, but if Austin seeks me out I shall certainly not rebuff him.'

'I'm not asking you to do that,' he replied impatiently. 'All I want is for you to use a little common sense and discretion.' He put his hands on her shoulders. 'Is it too much to ask? Does he mean so very much to you?'

Looking up into his eyes shadowed by the thick moisture-beaded lashes, Alex felt suddenly deflated. He was right, of course, her first duty was to their passengers. 'I'm sorry.' She spoke so quietly he had to bend his head to hear. 'I'll try not to be unreasonable.'

He smiled then, and the change was more than Alex could bear. When he was angry she could face up to him, but now—if he carried on looking at her so tenderly she would burst into tears.

'He'll be all yours when the trip's over,' he said softly. 'Try to be patient, Alexandra.'

She turned away desperately. 'You don't understand.'

'I think I do.'

But Alex knew that he didn't, and it seemed unlikely that he ever would.

CHAPTER SIX

For the next few days everything went according to plan. For a while Harry was shunned by the rest of the holidaymakers, but gradually they forgot the trouble he had caused and were once again one happy party.

Although Juliet was still frequently in Björn's company, Alex noticed that he now tried to mix whenever he could. She had seen Juliet's expression on one such occasion when he asked Valerie and Brian to join them, but Björn himself seemed unaware of her displeasure. Austin, too, often wandered away on one of his geological missions, as he termed them, so Alex's problem was solved so far as seeing very much of him was concerned.

Björn's attitude towards her had also undergone a subtle change. He seemed a little more tolerant, as though he was aware of the strain this holiday put on her. She knew he surmised that she was in love with Austin, and it seemed best to allow him to go on thinking this.

By the ninth day Alex had been lulled into a false sense of security, and was quite unprepared for the events which were about to take place. The whole day was to be spent exploring the surroundings of the box volcano Askja, which rose out of the great lava wastes of the Odádahraun north of Vatnajökull.

This grim desert waste of lava field was the realm of legendary fears and Alex, who had always been highly imaginative, could not help casting round furtive glances for the trolls or outlaws reputed to haunt this place. Austin laughed at her fears, but she noticed he never went far away and was always there when she needed him.

It was as they began their climb up the black slopes of Askja itself that Alex swore she saw something to their right. 'It was a man watching us,' she said to Austin, 'he was dressed in ragged old clothes and had a gun in his hand.'

Austin laughed. 'If there was such a person, where is he now?'

'He's hidden by a dip,' she insisted.

'You're imagining it,' he scoffed. 'But if it will make you feel any better, I'll go and take a look. Are you coming?'

She nodded. Still afraid, but with an urgent curiosity to discover whether her eyes had been playing tricks, she took his hand as he led her towards the spot where she had seen the shape.

By this time the remainder of the party were well ahead. 'Don't worry,' said Austin, seeing her take a fretful glance in their direction, 'we'll soon catch them up.'

They walked several hundred yards without seeing anyone and were about to turn back when a small boy appeared, pointing a toy pistol towards them and shouting wildly.

It was a relief for Alex to know that her eyes had not been deluding her, but where had he come from? There was no one else in sight.

He stopped a few yards away and looked fearlessly at them, his gun still at the ready. He wore blue jeans and a brown anorak, the hood fastened tightly round his chin. On top of this was perched a shabby stetson, and from his stance he had obviously watched many cowboy films.

Alex laughed and ran forward, kneeling down before him. His blue eyes looked steadily back. He was certainly not shy.

'Where are your parents?' she asked first in Icelandic and then English, but when he looked blankly back she tried again in French and Italian, and finally German. At last she got some response.

'*Sie sind dort*,' he laughed, and pointed down the slope, but when they looked there was no one to see.

She looked at Austin. 'We must try to find them. We can't leave him, he can't be more than four or five.'

'True. Perhaps we won't take long. Come on, young man,' and he lifted him on to his shoulders, 'let's see if we can find your mummy and daddy.'

'He doesn't seem afraid,' said Alex, as the child clung gleefully to Austin's head. 'They can't be far away.'

'You know what kids are like,' he replied, 'they wander away with no idea of distance. His parents could be anywhere. Suppose they've gone searching for him in the opposite direction; we might never find them.'

'Perhaps we ought to take him back to the coach?' wondered Alex.

'We'll try over here first,' Austin said, 'but if we have no success then I'm afraid we'll have to.'

'What's your name?' Alex asked the boy next, as she jogged along beside them.

'Franz,' he replied promptly.

'I'm Alex,' she said, 'and this is Austin.'

He repeated the names experimentally, and then as if suddenly remembering, '*Meine Mutti! Meine Mutti!*'

'He wants his mother,' said Alex. 'He must have just realised he's lost. I wonder if they've come by coach, or whether they're travelling alone?'

'I didn't see any other coaches,' said Austin, 'but I should ask him. I tell you one thing, he's no lightweight for his age.'

She found out that Franz and his parents were staying in Akureyri and had made the trip out to Askja for the day. Their car was a blue Beetle, hired for the holiday.

'It could be parked anywhere in the Odádahraun,' said Austin. 'I think we've set ourselves an impossible task.'

By this time Franz was crying, and when Austin wanted to put him down he steadfastly refused to let go. '*Mutti, Mutti!*' he called, while looking at Alex imploringly.

'We'll find her soon,' she reassured, wishing she had a biscuit or a sweet to pacify him. 'Where did you come from, over there? or over here?'

But whichever way she pointed she received an emphatic. '*Ja, ja,*' so she knew it was hopeless asking Franz. They would have to rely on their own judgment.

This particular area had been used as a training ground for American astronauts for their moon landing programme, and Alex knew that Austin had looked forward to climbing Askja with its steaming craters marking the way to the top and the lake inside. Now he was compelled to trudge across a desert of fine grit and cracked lava, in what seemed a futile effort to find young Franz's parents.

The boy had stopped crying, and when Alex looked again his eyes were closed. His head drooped drunkenly on his chest and traces of tears stained his cheeks.

'You can stop now,' whispered Alex, 'the poor little mite's asleep.'

She reached up and gently lifted him down and they laid him on the ground. 'He won't hurt for a minute,' said Austin, 'while I regain my strength. The lad's heavier than he looks.'

'What are we going to do? His parents must be frantic,' Alex said.

'They should have kept a better watch on him,' came the terse reply. 'It's Franz I'm concerned about, not his parents—all alone in this unfamiliar country. It's strange there's not a soul about. Is it always like this?'

'Oh no, but it's early in the season. Come high summer the place will be alive with people, relatively speaking, of course.'

'Then I prefer it now,' he said, 'except when we've got a lost boy to take care of. I think we'd best head back to camp, it seems pretty pointless wandering round and round.'

Alex nodded, not daring to say that she had lost all sense of direction. But when Austin swung Franz up into his arms and began walking she felt better. He must know the way, she thought, and followed confidently. It was not until he stopped and looked around that she knew she was wrong.

'What's the matter?' her voice was apprehensive.

'I thought this was the way,' he replied, 'but it can't be. The sun should be behind us, unless we've gone round in a circle.'

'I don't think we've done that,' said Alex. 'I—I think it's over there.'

He seemed not to notice her hesitation. 'Good girl. I'd forgotten you knew the place.' But after they had walked a quarter of a mile Alex knew that her guess had been wrong. Her anxiety was doubled by the knowledge that Björn was going to take a very dim view of this incident; coming on top of everything else she would be lucky if she kept her job. He would probably drop her off at the next town and tell her to find her own way back to Reykjavik. She wouldn't blame him, although until now none of the mishaps had been of her own making. This time it was her fault, but if she hadn't decided to look for her 'ghost' they would never have found Franz, who would be wandering alone now on the volcano, crying and lost and calling for his mother. He might never have been found! It didn't bear thinking about.

Björn's wrath, however, was something different altogether. She could almost imagine the cold grey eyes piercing into her very soul; destroying every shred of confidence. And his voice would be cold and accusing, leaving her in no doubt as to his feelings.

'Are you sure it's this way?' Austin's voice made her jump involuntarily.

'I—I thought it was—now I don't know. Oh, Austin, we're lost as well! What are we to do?'

There was a break in Alex's voice not entirely due to their unenviable position. Thoughts of Björn were still uppermost, and his reaction was what bothered her most.

'Alex—you're not crying?' He looked at her suspiciously. 'You're perfectly safe with me. If we don't turn up Björn will send out a search party, as he did with the Griffins. It's just a matter of deciding whether to stop here and wait or carry on trying.'

'We must keep on,' Alex's voice rose shrilly, 'I can't hang about doing nothing.'

Austin stopped and put Franz down again before taking Alex by the shoulders. 'Pull yourself together, it's not that bad. Or is it Björn who's upsetting you?' and as she nodded, 'I thought as much. You are a silly. He won't blame you this time. We couldn't leave the child to fend for himself.'

'We could have gone straight back to camp, or even taken him with us and followed the others.'

'It's easy to talk now,' he said soothingly, 'We did neither of those things, so it's no use distressing yourself. Once he realises there's a child involved he'll say nothing to you.'

'I'd like to think so,' she admitted.

She looked so miserable that Austin took her into his arms and held her close. 'My sweet, silly little Alex. How you do let that man deflate you!'

'Wouldn't you—if you loved him?'

His eyes rolled upwards. 'Heaven forbid, but I know what you mean. If you spurned my friendship, I should feel as despondent as you do now. As it is I shall never give up hope until it's too late.'

'And when will that be?' She felt a little better now, and managed a smile.

'When you're married to Björn,' he replied.

She laughed then. 'You must be joking! That's as remote a possibility as jumping over the moon.'

'Then you see there's still a chance for me,' and he gave her one of his sincere warm smiles, his brown eyes pleading eloquently.

Alex lifted her head and kissed him lightly. 'You're nice, Austin—far too nice for me. I get you into all sorts of trouble, yet you don't mind, you're ready to back me up whenever I need you. Who knows? I may yet decide to turn to you.'

'And I'll be ready and waiting when you do.'

The sound of Franz waking brought them back to the present. He rubbed his eyes with his fists and looked so tiny and defenceless that with a murmur of concern Alex bent down and gathered him into her arms. He nestled close for a moment before realising that she was not his mother, then he stood up and ran a few steps away, looking guardedly at them both.

'He's still half asleep,' cried Alex. 'Oh, why don't his parents come? He's so scared.'

'I would be too in his place.' Austin looked about him. 'All this lava and ash—it's so weird. He must think he's on another planet.'

Alex laughed. 'He wouldn't know what a planet is, he's too young. But I agree, it must be terrifying.' She held out her hand and timidly Franz took it. 'We mustn't let him see that we're lost too,' and to the child, 'Are you better now you've had a nice sleep?'

He nodded, but called again for his mother.

'We'll find her in a minute,' she assured him, and Franz trotted along beside her, seemingly confident that it was now only a matter of time before his parents were found.

It was in fact several hours. Hours spent retracing steps, stopping to take bearings and then ending up where they'd started. Alex was footsore and hungry —the boy too, though he did not complain. Austin had turned the search into a game of cowboys and Indians, and they had run up and down slopes chanting war-cries and hiding in crevices and caverns in the lava which were probably used by the outlawed heroes of the past.

Suddenly Franz darted away. *'Papa! Mutti!'* He had seen them before either Alex or Austin. Following behind them were Björn and Harry, and even at this distance Alex could see the forbidding lines on Björn's face.

Franz's parents were overjoyed at finding their son and could not thank Alex and Austin enough. 'He must have run away while we were looking through our binoculars,' said Herr Scholz. 'One minute he was there, and the next gone. We've searched and searched; my poor wife's nearly out of her mind with worry. It was by pure accident that we stumbled across your party, and Mr Einarsson here was so good.'

Björn gave a curt nod. 'I did what I could. After all, you are strangers to my country. May I give you a word of advice? Don't attempt any more trips unless you have an experienced guide—and put a pair of reins on that child!'

The Scholzes were so happy that they did not notice the asperity in his tone, but Alex was only too aware of it, and edged nearer to Austin. Her turn would come and she did not relish the thought. Austin squeezed her hand and she slanted him a weak smile, knowing as she did so that Björn watched—and condemned. He gave the Scholzes directions on how to reach their car, and after expressing their thanks they parted company.

The walk back was in silence, though Björn's disapproval showed in every line of his body. The proud tilt of his head, the straight lines of his back, all told Alex that this big man was annoyed. He was too polite to show his vexation in front of Harry, but Alex knew it was only a matter of time before the bomb exploded.

She was right. As soon as the bus came into sight he allowed Harry and Austin to go on ahead; his voice was cool but controlled.

'I appreciate your desire to help a child in distress, but surely it would have been wiser to call me without wandering away on your own?'

How could she tell him that at first sight she had not known it was a boy? That the tales of being haunted by outlaws as told by her grandfather when she was a child had become so real to her in this place that she had gone chasing after an apparition? 'We came across him by accident,' she said before realising her mistake.

He frowned. 'That makes matters even worse. I ought to have known you would try and slip away with Maddison while no one was looking.'

'You misjudge me,' she said bitterly, 'though I guess you wouldn't believe the truth even if I told you!'

'I think I've made a fair assessment of the situation,' he returned coldly. 'We'll come to that later. What bothers me at the moment is why you didn't ask for help.'

'Young Franz thought he knew where his parents were. The obvious thing seemed to try and find them.'

'So you spent hours and hours searching in vain. Whereas if you'd contacted me I would have known exactly what to do.'

He looked at her condescendingly down the length of his nose, and Alex felt her lower lip tremble ominously. He spoke again. 'You did intend coming back?'

'Of course,' she responded. 'We were on our way.'

'Heading in the wrong direction? You might as well admit it, you were lost too. You're very irresponsible, Alexandra.'

Alex glared at him then. 'Is that all you can think of, that I'm to blame? Can't you think of the child?'

'The boy's all right. Children are easily adaptable. He probably enjoyed playing games with you.'

So he had seen them long before they saw him! But it didn't alter the fact that he blamed her, and had dismissed Franz as though he were of no importance. She stopped and stamped her foot angrily.

'The trouble with you, Herra Einarsson, is that you have no heart. You're hard and cruel and don't care who you hurt so long as everything goes the way you want it to. How can you expect a holiday of this kind to run smoothly, with no mishaps? It would be a miracle if it did.'

His eyes glinted as he took a step closer, and for one moment Alex thought he was going to hit her. She closed her eyes. Björn in this mood frightened her; she had never seen him quite so angry. She held her breath and waited.

'I hope you didn't mean those words, Alexandra,' he said tartly. 'I may appear hard to you, but this is my living now, don't forget. And I'm trying to ensure that it's a success.'

He fought to control his feelings and Alex admired him for it. He was not accustomed to such blunt speaking. 'Censuring me won't help,' she said, 'I honestly did what I thought best. How was I to know that we'd lose our way too?'

They glared at each other for a moment like fighting cocks, then all at once he relaxed and shook his head. 'I must admit you've got spirit. I'll forgive you for the lost child episode, but I can't find it so easy to dismiss your wandering away with Maddison. Was there any motive behind it?'

It was now or never, thought Alex. She might as well tell him the truth, otherwise he would assume the worst and probably tackle Austin as well. She cleared her throat. 'Being an Icelander you might just about believe me, but when I was a child my grandfather used to enchant me with tales of trolls, and other things that lived here in the Odádahraun.'

He looked sceptical. 'You're not trying to tell me you saw one of these little people?'

'Not exactly, but I thought I saw a bandit.'

He nodded solemnly. 'I see—the legendary outlaws who used to try and make their living here. Did you find one?'

He was mocking her now, but Alex was still on the defensive. 'I'm truly serious—I did see something. I realised afterwards that it was only young Franz in his cowboy hat, but at a distance he——'

Björn's throaty chuckle interrupted her. 'Alexandra, you really are the limit! Why I put up with you I don't know.'

'But you do believe me?' Suddenly it was vital to know this. 'I'm not trying to wriggle out of my responsibilities, I know exactly how much this first trip means to you—and I'm honestly doing my best. I know it's not good enough for you—but you must believe that I'm trying.'

His anger had gone. The smoky eyes were human again, crinkling at the corners as he smiled. 'Do I have any option? You put up a very convincing argument.'

'So you'll accept the fact that I had no ulterior motive in deserting you?'

'Is it so important?' he questioned.

She nodded.

'In that case I do.'

By now they had reached the bus. Their disappearance had caused quite a stir, and it was easy to see that most people had thought along the same lines as Björn, until they heard about the lost child. There were now murmurs of sympathy as Alex told her story; only Björn stood on the outside, and she knew that he had not really believed her.

Later, lying beneath her canvas roof, Alex pondered on the man who had come to mean so much to her, so completely at variance with her idea of the man whom she would ultimately fall in love with and marry. Marry! Austin's suggestion amused her. Björn would never in a million years consider her as a wife. So far as he was concerned she was nothing more than a scatterbrained youngster with no idea of responsibility. But she would show him. For the rest of the tour her behaviour would be beyond reproach—she hoped. How many times had she said this and on each occasion failed—usually through no fault of her own?

This time, however, she would take extra care to see that nothing happened to ruin this promise she had made herself, for he might not be so lenient again. It was strange how he'd suddenly appeared to forget his anger; he was so unpredictable. Life would never be dull living with Björn, for his moods were as variable as the English weather, unless it was only with her that he lost his temper. He was very patient and forbearing with the rest of the party— except Harry, of course, when he was lost. She sympathised with Harry now. It could be very frightening not knowing whether you were going to be found or not, especially when you were miles from civilisation.

Alex then began to wonder what life would be

like, married to Björn. She had previously never allowed her thoughts to run in this direction, as the chances of it ever happening were so remote, but now her thoughts ran freely on. Would he be a good, kind and patient husband, tolerant and understanding, or had she got her priorities wrong? Did these things really matter? Wouldn't love disregard any faults he might possess, any irritating habits—wouldn't these failings, in the eyes of love, have a charm all of their own?

The fact that she loved Björn despite his overbearing manner proved this to be the case. If he returned her love she would be prepared to put up with his somewhat Victorian attitude; it was ironical when she recalled that she had strongly resented these same traits in Gerard. It proved that all the years she thought she was in love she had been mistaken. There was really no comparison between the two of them. Gerard was insignificant beside Björn. Björn's strength of character, his determination to get out of life exactly what he wanted, made him the mightier man and despite herself Alex admired him for it.

At breakfast the next morning Austin sought Alex out. 'What did Björn say? I expected him to tackle me, but he's said nothing yet.'

Alex shrugged. 'He was pretty mad to start with, and I was annoyed with him because he didn't seem to care about the child—I think he enjoys using me as his whipping-boy. Anyway, in the end he was all right. It amused him to think that I believe all the old stories of trolls and giants. It probably confirmed his belief that I'm still a child.'

Austin laughed. 'You should grow a bit, then he might change his mind. Now me, I like my girls tiny. It brings out the protective instinct.'

'It's the story of my life,' she grumbled, 'being treated as an infant. How I long to be tall and willowy!'

He snorted. 'Not all men like tall girls.'

'Björn does. Look how he's always round Juliet.' The blonde was almost as tall as Björn himself, and to Alex this only emphasised the difference in their height. How could he avoid treating her as a child when there was someone as elegant as Juliet around?

Austin shook his head impatiently. 'Haven't you noticed it's nearly always Juliet who does the running? She's the same with me.'

'I don't see either of you avoiding her,' Alex retorted, 'in fact you seem to enjoy her company.'

'She can be very entertaining, and also she's extremely interested in all aspects of the tour. She's always asking questions.'

Alex considered this. 'I wonder if it has any bearing on her being here? It's odd, her travelling alone. It doesn't fit, somehow.'

'Austin nodded. 'I agree, though I can't imagine what she has in mind.'

At that moment, almost as though she knew they were discussing her, Juliet walked across. Björn, Alex noticed, was poring over some papers in the bus, so no doubt Juliet felt neglected.

'May I join you?' she asked, and without waiting for an answer perched herself on a rounded piece of lava next to Austin. 'That was a smart move,' she said, nudging him. 'How'd you manage to get away with it?'

'What are you talking about?' he looked mystified.

'You know very well,' she smirked. 'And you, Alex, I'm surprised at you. Didn't you know Björn frowns on such goings-on?'

Alex lifted her fine brows and tried to look cool, though inside she was seething. It was easy to see how Juliet's mind worked. 'Perhaps you haven't heard all the story? Austin and I found a small lost child and spent all afternoon trying to locate his parents.'

Juliet waved her hand airily. 'Oh, I heard that, but you don't expect me to believe it? After all, we didn't see the boy, and I know how difficult it is to get any time alone. Björn and I *always* seem to be interrupted.'

Alex was in no doubt that she was referring to herself, but ignoring the innuendo she said, 'You have a foul mind, Juliet. If you don't believe us, ask Björn. He saw the child.'

'I already have, but how do I know he's not shielding you? After all, it wouldn't do for our courier's good name to be smeared, now would it?'

Alex was about to tell Juliet exactly what she thought of her when Austin spoke. 'Juliet! I'm surprised at you. I didn't think you capable of such unkind thoughts.'

'It's not only me who thinks that—ask any of the others,' she cried, realising her mistake and trying to excuse herself. 'They were all talking about you.'

'Maybe so,' snapped Alex, 'but they believed us when they found out the truth.'

'So they let you think, but I won't argue any more. I've made my point,' and Juliet wandered away as calmly as though nothing had happened.

Alex was furious. 'If I hadn't my position to consider I wouldn't have let her get away with that!'

'She's jealous,' remarked Austin.

'Why? It's easy to see Björn prefers her.'

'But she's not sure of him,' he insisted. 'Even though our little plan has had a certain amount of success she's still uncertain.'

Unconvinced, Alex said, 'How I hate that woman! Why did she come?'

Austin placed his hand on her arm. 'Between her and Björn you're getting yourself worked up into a fine state! Forget them. Take each day as it comes. Do the best you can and I'm sure things will turn out in the end.'

'What would I do without you? You're right as usual, I'm being silly. I don't know what's come over me.'

'Love,' he said softly, 'it's made you more perceptive. I feel the same way towards you.'

'Then why didn't you stick up for me?' she asked.

'If I'd jumped to your defence it would have confirmed her suspicions.'

'I suppose so,' Alex agreed glumly.

'Don't look so miserable, then. I'm on holiday,

don't forget, and I want cheerful company, not someone who looks as though she's lost a fortune.'

She smiled ruefully. 'Forgive me, I didn't mean to be a wet blanket.'

'You'll never be that. Now, what have we planned for today?'

'More swimming, at Lake Mývatn, but first of all we go to Námaskard. That should interest you. The area's full of quagmires and fumaroles and boiling sulphur pits.'

Björn was silent as they started their journey, and Alex wondered whether he still dwelled on yesterday's episode. He had said he accepted her explanation, but she could still feel his annoyance. She glanced obliquely at him: he gave no indication that he was aware of her interest, but he must know, she thought, and unable to bear the uncomfortable silence any longer she said, 'Is anything the matter?'

It was the wrong question to ask a man of Björn's type and she ought to have known it. 'Should there be?' He didn't even look at her.

'You—you seem strange this morning. I thought perhaps you were still cross.'

'I've already forgotten,' he said stiffly. 'I'm just wondering what's going to happen next.'

She stiffened. 'That's not a very nice thing to say. Do you think I go round looking for trouble?'

'Not exactly, but you do seem to attract it. I wish I'd followed my first instincts. I can't say you've been exactly useful.'

'I've done my best,' retorted Alex hotly, 'if that's not good enough I don't know what is.'

'I'm not decrying your aptitude as a guide. You know the island almost as well as I do, and you have an ability to make everything sound interesting. It's not that, it's your general behaviour. I suppose I should have known you'd lose your head over some fellow.'

'I have not lost my head, as you term it!' hissed Alex, aware that their conversation was arousing interest at the back of the bus. 'Why do you insist on trying to blacken my character?'

The glance he threw her was both amused and tolerant. 'I only know what my eyes tell me. If you want to maintain your good reputation you should be more discreet in your affairs.'

Alex remained silent, trying to calm her thoughts. It was painful being told by the man you loved that you were useless, that he would have done better without you. It made her feel like giving up. Maybe that was what he had in mind—it would save him sacking her. This idea renewed her determination to prove she was not the frivolous person he thought.

'I'm sorry if I've offended you,' she said evenly. 'It won't happen again.'

He didn't look at her, but she could tell that he was highly sceptical of her promise.

'I really mean it,' she persisted, 'I took this job with every intention of proving that you were wrong when you declared it unsuitable for a woman. I had hoped you'd find me good enough to ask me to stay on.'

He laughed, a short dry laugh that held no amusement. 'Heaven forbid! And have you hankering after every eligible male who came your way?'

'Now you're being unfair,' she exclaimed.

'Am I? What do you expect me to think? You run away from one man straight into the arms of another, and then you tell me that you're merely friends. What's to stop me thinking that you would make *friends* with anyone else who came along?'

Tears pricked her eyes. He was being unnecessarily cruel, but she mustn't let him see how much he hurt her. She was quite sure that weakness was one thing he despised in a woman. 'I'm sorry that's how you feel. I can see it's no use my protesting any longer. All I can say is that you're badly mistaken.'

'I hope I am,' he said surprisingly. 'I'd like nothing better than to be proved wrong.'

That was something, thought Alex. Perhaps things were not as bad as they looked.

They were approaching Námaskard now. The ground here was brown streaked with yellow and green and encrusted white along the fissures, with steam rising or shooting out in sharp jets. They drove past a notice which read 'Keep out' in English. 'No one ever does,' said Björn when she looked at him questioningly.

The colours were darker here, black and orange, brown and blue. On either side of the track the mud rose in heaving bubbles which grew and burst. Alex shivered. They looked as though they would like to reach out and pull down anyone who dared trespass too near. From the conversation at the back of the bus she knew that many others felt the same; they could smell the sulphorous odours. It was a soul-destroying place, and Alex was glad when they moved on.

'I see your fertile imagination was at work again,' Björn said, his lips twisting in amusement, 'I could almost see you shivering in terror. It surprises me that you want to live in Iceland.'

'It's the variety I like,' she said. 'Where else can you find glaciers and mountains, volcanoes and rivers? What do they call it—land of ice and fire? It's very true, and I love it.'

'It's also been called the mouth of Hell. Some time in the sixth century it's said that an Irish missionary and his companions sailed near to what they thought was a smoking mountain, and that the inhabitants threw lumps of burning clinker at them. They departed as quickly as they could, firmly believing they had neared the mouth of Hell.'

Alex laughed. 'Poor souls! I bet they never came near again. My grandfather used to tell me stories about Iceland, and I never knew whether to believe him or not.'

'I think you have to decide for yourself what is fact or fallacy. There are so many legends, like the one about the Westmann Isles being missiles hurled there by giant trolls. Do you believe that?'

'Now you're making fun of me,' she protested, but she didn't mind. She would far rather have Björn in this spirit than in one of his censorious moods.

It looked, thought Alex, like being a good day after all ... How wrong she was!

CHAPTER SEVEN

Two nights were being spent at Lake Mývatn, a veritable paradise for the nature-lover, and although Alex had visited the lake many times she never tired of this northern area of Iceland.

Camp was set up and after lunch the holiday-makers were free to explore at will. Most of them expressed a preference to bathe in the natural hot water pools in underground caves on the north-eastern side of the lake, and for a time Alex was alone with Björn. Austin had persuaded Juliet to accompany him, and Alex guessed he had done it expressly to leave her a clear field with her employer.

Björn quirked an eyebrow. 'No swimming?'

'Not yet,' smiled Alex. 'I feel lazy.'

'I'm not surprised after yesterday.'

She looked at him suspiciously, but he smiled. 'How about taking out a boat? It doesn't look as though we'll be needed for a while.'

He couldn't know how her heart leapt at the prospect; it was more than she had dared hope to spend some time alone with him. She wondered if Juliet, had she known what Björn had in mind, would have gone off quite so happily with Austin. The thought brought a smile to her face.

'That would be lovely. Grandfather never took me

on the lake as he said the effort of rowing was too much for him—and he wouldn't let me try.'

'I'll teach you if you like—if you're really interested?'

'Oh, would you?' said Alex eagerly.

'If you promise to do exactly as I tell you and not try anything silly,' he qualified.

'I promise,' she nodded.

And so it was settled.

It was a perfect day for idling about on the water. The sun shone out of a cloudless sky, and Alex felt happier than she had for a long time. Björn was an expert rower, as she might have expected, and the next hour passed very pleasantly. They made small-talk, but for most of the time Alex was content to relax and enjoy this idyllic summer day. It was nice to pretend that there had never been anything wrong between her and Björn, that always there had been this rapport.

Waterfowl of many different species glided silently out of their path, and once away from the shore it was almost as though they were in a world of their own. A peaceful world, the silence broken only by the splash of the oars and the occasional calling of a bird. Later there would be other boats on the lake, but for the present it was theirs, and Alex knew that this was one of the moments she would treasure long after the tour was over.

Her eyelids drooped with the rhythmic effect of the oars until Björn's voice suddenly aroused her.

'Your turn now, before you drop off to sleep.'

148

'I wasn't,' she protested, laughing, 'I was merely enjoying this unexpected interlude.'

'I'm glad,' he said softly, so softly that Alex wondered whether she had imagined it. 'Come and sit by me. We'll take an oar each until you know what you're doing.'

She looked at him wide-eyed, and was about to refuse when she realised he would think it strange. But once she was seated beside him, their bodies touching and his hands over hers as he showed her how to hold the oar, Alex's pulses accelerated to such an extent that she was sure he must hear the pounding of her heart. Her mouth felt suddenly dry and she had difficulty in answering when he asked if she understood.

'I—I think so,' and she attempted to pull her oar through the water as he had instructed. At first she went in too deep and found it almost impossible to move the oar, but after a few experimental strokes she began to get the idea and before long was rowing evenly beside her partner.

'You're doing very well,' he said a few minutes later. 'Would you like to try by yourself now? Your arms might not be long enough, but——'

'I'd love to,' she cut in, more to get him away from her than anything else. It had been sheer torture sitting beside him trying to remain indifferent; every fibre of her being called out to him and she was afraid he might notice and ask what was wrong. Darling Björn, her heart called, why is it that you do these things to me? Why do I ache to have you hold me in your arms and whisper words

149

of love? Why do you appear so indifferent to my need of you?

And then the impossible happened.

Almost as though he had heard her silent appeal she felt his arm about her shoulders. When she looked at him there was a strange light in his eyes and his head bent closer to hers, blotting out the surrounding landscape. A muffled cry escaped her lips as his mouth closed over hers; she fought for a second, her mind wildly seeking the reason for his actions. She meant nothing to him—why was he doing this? And then she gave up questioning and allowed herself to respond in the way her whole body desired. Later she would try and work out why he acted this way, but now ... she was drowning in the sweet ecstasy of her love, returning kiss for kiss, not caring what he thought of her reactions.

His kiss was both passionate and brutal, and her lips felt bruised. This was not the way she had imagined he would make love, but she was past caring. Here in the arms of the man she loved time stood still, church bells pealed and angels in heaven sang.

She was totally unprepared when he let her go, clinging involuntarily to him until she saw the expression on his face. Instead of the torment of love which she felt sure must be mirrored in her own eyes, there was revulsion. Her hand flew to her mouth. 'W-what's the matter? Why do you look at me so?'

'It's what I expected,' he grated harshly. 'How free you are with your *love*.' He said the word distastefully. 'Are you the same with Austin and Gerard—no, don't answer, I know. I'd hoped you'd prove me wrong.' He actually looked hurt for a few seconds before his eyes hardened. 'I should have known better than to expect anything different.'

Alex sat in shocked silence. All she could do was stare at him. Why was he saying these things? What did he mean? Couldn't he tell that she loved him, hadn't her unpremeditated response told him as much?

Suddenly she dropped her head in her hands. She couldn't bear to see the loathing on his face and knew she could go on with this journey no longer. He'd never believe her if she tried to explain. There was nothing for it but to return to Helga and Jón, and later to England. A bus service ran between Mývatn and Akureyri, and from there she could fly to Reykjavik. Within hours there would be over four hundred kilometres between her and this man who seemed to delight in humiliating her.

She felt him move, and when she looked up saw that he had taken the seat she had recently vacated. 'Have I put you to shame?' he said smoothly. 'Didn't you think I'd guess what type of woman you are?'

Alex glared at him. 'And hasn't it ever occurred to you that you might be wrong?'

'How can I be,' he voice derisive now, 'when you've given me no cause to think otherwise?'

'You mean you won't admit it? You've put your own interpretation on my actions and nothing will make you change your mind?'

Why was she arguing, why didn't she confess that

she loved him? Why allow him to deride her so? But she knew that the answer to these questions was pride. How could you tell a man you loved him when he had given you no encouragement, when every word and every action showed that he had no interest? She might as well admit there could never be anything between them. She was doing the right thing in leaving. To stay would only bring more heartache.

'Try giving me an explanation,' he said drily. 'Though I must warn you, it will need to be very plausible before I'm convinced.'

'Then there's no point in trying,' she flashed. 'I have no wish to make a further fool of myself.'

She picked up the oars, anger adding strength to her actions, and began rowing furiously back towards the shore. Her movements were erratic and her course far from straight, but she didn't care, and when Björn called out wildly for her to stop she ignored him.

'Pull on your right, pull on your right!' he repeated, and at last the urgency in his tone reached through to her, and with a swift glance behind she saw that they were heading for a small island overgrown with shrubs and trees. Too late she tried to correct her course, the boat grazed the banks and an outstretched branch knocked her forward against Björn. As though in slow motion Alex felt the boat overturning. She grabbed wildly at the air before the freezing waters closed over her head. Down—and up again, gasping for air. Björn was already reaching out for the capsized boat, and she swam after him. 'I'm sorry, I had no idea——'

He stopped her with a glance. 'Sorry! Trouble should be your middle name. I might have known something like this would happen!'

'How was I to know this island was behind me? I thought I was heading for the shore.'

'If you'd listened instead of going your own hot-headed way you'd have avoided it. What was the matter? Couldn't you stand a few home truths?'

She was at his side now and glared indignantly, her wet hair clinging sleekly to her head and shoulders like the fur of a seal, and sparkling beads of water suspended from her eyelashes and eyebrows. 'If you were justified I shouldn't mind, but when you insist on putting your own construction on things, then I do take offence.'

'You sound very convincing,' he panted, struggling to right the upturned boat, 'I almost feel like believing you.' He paused in his struggles and looked at her for a moment. 'Why *did* you kiss me like that? If I didn't know better I'd be inclined to believe that you liked me a little.'

A *little*! her heart cried out. I love you! If only you'd show some interest then perhaps I could tell you how I feel. As things stood, however, what could she say? She turned away in despair. There was no answer. She would have to let him go on believing that she responded to every man in the same way.

His voice taunted her. 'Now what's the matter? Are you trying to think of a plausible excuse?'

Alex was glad he couldn't see her tears. She swallowed painfully, searching for the right words that would make him forget this argument, and was totally unprepared when he twisted her round in the water to face him.

His eyes narrowed. 'Typical feminine reaction when they don't know how to get out of a situation,' he sneered, 'at least it's proved me right. Give me a hand with the boat and let's get back to camp before we catch our death of cold.'

In the heat of her temper Alex had not realised how cold the water was, but once in the boat with her trousers and sweater clinging icily to her body she could not control her chattering teeth or shivering limbs.

The boatkeeper muttered something about fooling about in the boat, and Alex was afraid to speak in case Björn insulted her again.

Their tents had already been erected, so Alex was able to change in privacy. She felt deeply humiliated that Björn should think her a loose woman, and was more firmly convinced than ever that no good could come of her continuing this tour. How could she do her best when Björn was continually observing her, ready to pick on her at the slightest excuse? Why did she love him? *Why?*

She was so long in her tent that Björn came looking to see what was the matter.

'Are you all right?'

She jumped guiltily at the sound of his voice, afraid he had read her thoughts. Her face turned scarlet as she stared at him. 'Of course I am. Why shouldn't I be?' and she sneezed.

'I hope you haven't caught a chill—you look very flushed.' He opened the flap further and crawled in beside her.

Alex backed away. There was so little room it was impossible to avoid contact. Their knees touched as they faced each other—Alex on her guard like a cornered animal and Björn as though he were about to pounce. He raised his hand and she tensed herself, waiting, somewhat surprised when he placed it on her forehead. She felt herself grow warm beneath his touch and held her breath, trying to still the thudding of her heart.

'As I thought,' he said, 'you feel as though you're running a temperature. I'll fetch you some aspirin, but I think you ought to stay in bed for the next twenty-four hours, just to be on the safe side.'

Alex drew back and stared at him, her eyes round and luminous and slightly incredulous. 'I'm all right, I tell you. There's nothing wrong with me.' Except a broken heart—and staying in bed won't help that.

'I'd rather make sure,' he insisted. Dressed in black sweater and trousers he seemed to Alex, in her present hypersensitive mood, somehow menacing. 'The chap who runs the hotel here is a friend of mine, and I'm quite sure he'll have a spare room. Gather your things together while I find out.'

He had gone before she could protest. Matters were taken out of her hands; there was no chance now of running away. It was almost as though she were being kept prisoner. Had he any idea what was in her mind? Was he doing this purposely to foil her arrangements? But no, he couldn't possibly have guessed. Alex clenched her fists and banged them on the ground. She wasn't ill! Her dip had done her no harm, but how could she explain this? Every time he came near her temperature rose, did he but know it.

There was nothing for it but to fall in with his plans. A day in bed would at least keep her out of his way, and then he could blame her for no further incidents.

Resigned now, she pushed pyjamas and tooth-brush into her bag and waited his return. The sound of an aeroplane overhead reminded her that had things turned out differently she could have been on such a plane in the space of an hour or so. It was ironical the way things had turned out.

'It's all arranged. Magnar was delighted to help.'

Björn had returned. Meekly Alex followed him across the field towards the hotel. He seemed almost happy at the prospect of leaving her there, which thought only served to make her even more dismayed. It was quite obvious there could never be anything between them, and she was stupid to go on eating out her heart in this manner. It would be best to try and put him completely out of her mind. He thought she loved Austin, so why not confirm his suspicions and turn her affections to this kind Englishman? Austin himself would be only too pleased, and it would be one way of avoiding any more intimate scenes with Björn, which were disturbing to say the least. She still could not understand why he had decided to kiss her, for she was quite sure that it was not purely to find out what type of a woman she was. There must be some other reason behind his actions.

'Hang on to me if you feel groggy,' Björn said.

'It's all right,' she snapped, 'I don't know why you're making all this fuss. I'm quite sure there's nothing wrong with me.' She wouldn't admit that her legs felt weak and her head ached. It was reaction to Björn's presence, that was all. As soon as he had gone she would be better, and feel nothing but a fraud taking up a room in his friend's hotel.

The room to which they were shown was pleasantly furnished in shades of yellow and gold and had a marvellous view across the lake. After ensuring that everything was to her liking Björn left, with the strict instructions that she was to go straight to bed.

Alex undressed, but sat for a while on a chair near the window, wondering what the rest of the holiday-makers would think of her being confined to bed like this. During the journey she had struck up quite a friendship with most of the passengers, and she guessed they would all be concerned for her health. Only Juliet would put her own construction on the situation, no doubt thinking that Alex had some ulterior motive in being moved to the hotel. She would certainly surmise that Alex herself had engineered the whole thing in the hope that she would be able to get Björn to herself, but it was unlikely that he would visit her. Having done what he considered to be his duty, he would now feel free to enjoy himself, probably not thinking of Alex again until it was time for them to leave Lake Mývatn.

A waitress entered with a tray of food, but Alex shook her head. She didn't feel in the least hungry, and suddenly bed looked very inviting. When her legs almost gave way beneath her she began to think that perhaps Björn had been right in his diagnosis. Not that she would admit it—her eyes closed, her thoughts became blurred, and she slept.

When she woke she was surprised to find Austin sitting at her bedside. 'W—what are you doing here?' she whispered hoarsely.

He smiled and smoothed back the hair which had fallen untidily across her face. 'Looking after my girl. Björn told me what happened, so I came over straight away.'

'What time is it? Have I been asleep long?'

'Nearly ten. It certainly takes some getting used to, this continual daylight. But how are you, Alex? You had me worried—you've been so restless, and you're still hot. Shall I call a doctor?'

She smiled weakly. 'I think I've caught a chill—Björn was right. But I don't need a doctor, I'll be better tomorrow.' Her eyelids drooped heavily. It was almost too much effort to speak.

'Why does it always happen to you?' he whispered, leaning forward to press a kiss on her forehead.

Alex did not know that a third person had entered the room and stood silently watching. She accepted Austin's caress without demur. He really was a darling, and she said as much. 'Dearest Austin, you're so good to me.'

The door shut with a crash, causing them both to

look up, startled. Austin sprang to his feet and crossed the room, opening the door to look along the corridor.

'It was Björn,' he said sharply, returning to the bed. 'I wonder what construction he put on that?'

Alex knew, and should have felt relieved that her plan was beginning to take shape so quickly, but instead she felt more despondent than ever and could not stop the tears that welled.

Austin looked concerned. 'Please—nothing's ever so bad as it looks.'

'I can't help it.' Her voice was a mere whisper. 'But I'd like you to know that I've at last accepted the fact that Björn is not for me.'

'I'll help you.' Austin dropped to his knees beside the bed. 'I'll do all I can.'

Alex clung to his hand. 'Thank you, Austin, I'll try not to disappoint you.'

'You mean—you're prepared to'—and as she nodded—'oh, Alex! I'll make you truly happy, I promise. You'll never regret this day.'

It was done. Alex closed her eyes and tried to shut out the visions of Björn that floated in front of her. She would learn to love Austin in time—he would make a good husband, perhaps better than Björn—dearest Björn. And so her mind ran on until at last she fell into a fitful sleep. Even here she was not free from the torment of the Icelander. Wherever she went he was there; mocking, sneering, ready to decry her every action. Please go away, she cried, go away—and woke to the echo of her own voice.

She was alone. A glance at her watch showed that

it was two in the morning. Perspiration soaked her pyjamas and she pulled the sheets up closer round her neck. She sniffed—Björn's cigarettes! So he had been here recently! Why?

She tossed the question over and over in her mind without reaching any conclusion, and at length sleep again took over. This time she slept easily, and eight hours passed before she stirred once more. Almost immediately the waitress came in to inquire whether she would like something to eat. By now Alex felt much better and agreed that a light breakfast would be very acceptable.

As she ate the door opened and Björn appeared. He nodded and gave a tight-lipped smile. 'It's nice to see you looking better. How are you feeling?'

'All right, I think—though I haven't tried getting out of bed yet.'

He appeared uneasy, which was so unlike Björn that she said, 'It was nice of you to sit with me during the night. I hope it didn't inconvenience you.'

He looked at her sharply. 'I didn't realise you were aware of my presence.'

'Your cigarettes gave you away,' she told him, 'they have a very distinctive odour.'

'I hope the smoke didn't bother you. I never gave it a thought.'

Alex shook her head. Why were they talking like this, making polite conversation as though they were strangers? She sipped the coffee. Perhaps he felt uncomfortable because she was in bed? That must be it. Why else would he be so ill at ease? He was normally so confident, so assured.

She studied him as she drank. He had crossed to the window and stood looking out. She had seen this profile so many times on the journey as he sat behind the wheel. The smooth, high brow, the aquiline nose that made him appear proud and regal, the full mobile lips which were now pressed firmly together. Tall and straight, he gazed out over the lake though Alex guessed he did not see the picture before his eyes, and when he turned she was surprised by his expression. He looked—she couldn't quite make up her mind—worried? troubled?

Unconsciously she put out her hand. 'Björn, what's the matter?' She spoke hesitantly, almost afraid to ask. 'I hope I've not become a burden. If so, I—I'm quite prepared to return to Reykjavik.'

'Don't be silly!' His voice was sharp. 'Naturally I feel responsible for you and I promised Helga I'd look after you, but as for you leaving the party, that's nonsense. Unless you think you won't be well enough to travel?'

'Oh, I will, but I do seem to cause you a lot of trouble. You didn't have much sleep last night and you're here now when you could be enjoying yourself with Juliet.'

He looked startled. 'Why should I want to be with Juliet, for heaven's sake?'

'I thought that you and she were—friends?'

He shook his head impatiently. 'I try to be friends with everyone—that's my job, as it should be yours.'

'Meaning I've fallen down on the job?' she flashed.

'Not exactly, but you do seem to have fallen rather heavily for Maddison—despite all I've said.'

Here was her chance, yet still she hesitated.

'If you're thinking of denying it, I shouldn't bother,' he jeered. 'I took it upon myself to ask your friend exactly what his intentions were.'

Alex's head shot up. This wasn't the way she wanted him to find out. 'Of all the nerve! It has nothing to do with you. I hope Austin told you to mind your own business!'

'On the contrary,' he replied smoothly, 'he said that he plans to ask you to marry him when the holiday is over.'

'H-he said that?' She was surprised, to say the least. She thought Austin would have been a little more discreet. But on second thoughts, why should he? She had indicated that she was prepared to offer him more than just friendship, so why keep the news to himself? It was just that it was a shock hearing Björn repeat it like this.

'You sound surprised,' he observed. 'I can't think why.'

'I'm surprised he told you, that's all. Of course I knew he would ask me to marry him—it was only a matter of time.'

His eyebrows rose. 'So you'll be going back to England after all?'

'We haven't got that far. It will depend on Austin.'

'But you'll do whatever he says?' he insisted.

'Of course. Doesn't one always try to please the man one loves?' She felt a compulsive urge to get back at this man. She wanted to hurt him as she herself had been hurt. But of course that was impossible. He had no feelings. Whatever she said would make no difference, except to lower his estimation of her even more.

'I suppose that's the general idea,' he said, walking towards the door. 'I hope you'll both be very happy. No doubt he'll be up to see you later on. Is there any message you'd like me to give him?'

'No, thanks.'

'Not even your love?' his eyes narrowed meanfully.

'He knows how I feel,' she retorted.

'How touching,' he said quietly, and then he was gone, leaving Alex to bury her head despairingly in the pillow. She did not hear the door re-open, nor see Björn look questioningly at her. If she had she might have told him there and then how she felt; as it was she could only wonder why fate had decreed that she should be so unhappy. Surely she was entitled to more out of life than this eternal despondency?

To increase Alex's depression, Juliet decided to pay her a visit. She stood at the end of the bed looking down. 'I was sorry to hear that you'd caught a chill. How on earth did you manage to fall into the water? Björn said you were trying to row.' She arched her delicate brows scornfully.

'It was an unfortunate mistake,' Alex tried to keep her voice even, 'it could have happened to anyone.'

'I doubt if I would have been so silly if Björn had asked me to go rowing with him. Tell me, did he ask you, or was it your idea? When I asked him earlier what he was doing he said he had some repairs to do to the bus. That's why I went off with Austin—in case you're wondering.'

Alex was a little surprised by this statement as she had not seen Björn tinkering with the vehicle. In fact as soon as Juliet and Austin were out of sight he had invited her to join him, and it gave her great pleasure to tell Juliet this.

The blonde girl frowned. 'I wonder why, unless he'd decided to do it later. How did you persuade him to get you this room? It's very convenient, I must say.'

'And just what do you mean by that?' grated Alex.

'Don't think I haven't seen him coming and going,' Juliet snapped, 'and Austin too. Quite a little set-up you've made for yourself!'

'Get out,' spat Alex between gritted teeth. 'I don't have to put up with your insinuations.'

'I haven't finished yet.' Juliet observed Alex coolly. 'Is it true that you and Austin are engaged?'

'If you want the answer to that you'd better ask him yourself. Now get out before I ring for someone to come and put you out.'

Unperturbed, Juliet strolled towards the door. 'I shall certainly do that, don't worry. And I'd like to say that I think you're being very sensible. Björn just isn't your type.'

'And I suppose you think he's yours?' Alex could not resist asking.

'You might say we're two of a kind. If you stick around long enough you'll find out one day what I mean.' And she was gone, leaving Alex feeling slightly bewildered. What did she mean by that curious statement? How could they be two of a kind? Björn had none of Juliet's devious methods. He was honest and straightforward, and she was quite sure he had never had a malevolent thought in his life. All along she had thought there was something curious in Juliet making this trip, and now she was doubly sure. But she couldn't even hazard a guess as to what it might be.

She still felt puzzled when Austin put in an appearance. Her succession of visitors began to tire her out, and as if sensing this he did not stay long. After that Alex slept.

It was early evening when she woke again. This time she felt much better and decided it was time she returned to camp, but before she had even begun to take action Björn called in. When she told him her decision he instantly forbade her to leave the hotel. 'Another night's sleep here is what you need. It gets cold in the tents. I can't risk you catching pneumonia. In fact, I'm wondering whether it's advisable to let you finish the tour after all.'

'Björn—you must!' Faced with the thought of being able to go, Alex knew she didn't want to. There were only four more days before the holiday finished, and she suddenly knew that these would be the most precious days of the whole tour. After that it was unlikely she would ever see Björn again. 'I know I said I'd go back to Reykjavik, but I don't really want to. Despite everything, I'm enjoying myself.'

'That goes without saying,' drily, 'but if I could persuade Maddison to travel with you, perhaps you'd think differently?'

'No! You can't, I mean—you mustn't ruin his holiday. After all he's paid for this trip.'

'I'd give him a refund,' he offered.

Alex eyed him warily. 'Do you really want to get rid of me?' She sighed. 'If so, I suppose I have no choice.' She couldn't very well tell him that he was the reason she wanted to stay.

'We'll see how you feel in the morning,' he said abruptly, frowning at the sad expression which crossed her face. 'You're a funny child. I thought you'd jump at the opportunity of leaving me, especially if your boy friend went too.'

Child! Was that how he saw her? Didn't he realise she was a woman with all the feelings and desires peculiar to a woman in love? Had he no idea at all how she felt? She was perfectly sure that were the positions reversed she would be able to tell at once exactly what his feelings were.

'Perhaps it's my sense of honour,' she replied stiffly. 'Once a job's started I believe in seeing it through.'

'Very commendable, though I can't say you look exactly overjoyed at the idea of staying.'

'That's because I thought you didn't want me,' she blurted.

He looked astonished. 'What a peculiar thing to say! You're a big help to me—most of the time—but I can't risk you jeopardising your health purely out of a sense of duty.'

'Oh, do stop fussing! There's nothing wrong with me now. I've completely recovered.'

He laughed at her outraged expression. 'Okay, you win, but I'm going to leave instructions that you have no more visitors tonight—not even Austin.'

'Very well, sir,' said Alex primly, then she too laughed.

Björn remained for a further hour after that, and it was one of the happiest periods Alex had spent. They discussed all sorts of subjects and found they had a great deal in common. He was like a big brother, joking and teasing but showing concern and kindness. This was an entirely different side to his nature and endeared him even more to Alex's heart. She ached to put out her hand and touch him, to draw him close and feel his strength beside her. It was sweet agony sitting and talking as though he meant nothing to her when all the time she longed for his caresses.

Although she did not want this interlude to end it was something of a relief when he at last declared that he must go. She could stand his presence no longer without giving away her true feelings; indeed she felt sure he had only to look into her eyes to know how she felt. Surely her very soul was bared at that moment for him to see?

'Goodnight, Alexandra, sleep tight.' He bent over

the bed and dropped a light kiss on her forehead, turned abruptly as if he regretted it, and left the room without a backward glance.

Alex raised her hand and touched the spot where his kiss burned her skin. She felt bemused and gazed abstractedly at the door, still seeing his face as he bent over her. What was it she had seen, in that one unguarded second?

CHAPTER EIGHT

THE remainder of the tour passed quickly and uneventfully. Björn was kinder to Alex than he had ever been, but she could tell that he still regarded her as an employee and nothing more. Austin was her constant companion, and in a way this helped push her feelings for Björn to the back of her mind. It was only at night that she was unable to banish him from her thoughts. As she lay in the semi-darkness of her tent mental pictures passed before her mind's eye; almost always he was smiling and his eyes, those handsome eyes which had attracted her from the first moment they met, regarded her tenderly, almost lovingly. Just such an expression as she had seen on his face that day at the hotel. She had been mistaken, of course, but at night it gave her pleasure to lie and think what it would be like to be loved by this man.

The last day arrived. Back at Reykjavik Björn was

making his goodbyes. Transport had been arranged to take the passengers to the airport at Keflavik, but he was not going with them. He held out his hand to Alex and looked at her critically. 'You look as though you're feeling the strain of the past fourteen days. Make sure you have a good rest. Is it back to England now, or are you staying for a while?'

So—he was not offering her the job for a further period. Alex had not expected him to do so, but she couldn't help feeling hurt. Somewhere at the back of her mind she had cherished a hope that he might find her indispensable.

'I shall probably stay with Helga for a while, at least until Jón's properly better.'

Björn frowned. 'He's been ill?'

Alex expressed surprise. 'Didn't I tell you? He had an accident the day we started the tour.'

He looked puzzled for a moment. 'Is that why you were late? Why on earth didn't you say?'

'You were in no mood to listen,' she replied.

'And so you let me think you were at fault. I do wish you'd told me.'

'It doesn't matter now,' feeling suddenly warmed by his concern.

'To me it does. I don't like to find I've misjudged a person.' The smoky eyes looked kindly down. 'Believe me, I'm truly sorry.'

'Apology accepted,' said Alex lightly, 'I'm as much to blame for not telling you.'

'What happened to Jón?' he inquired.

'A hit-and-run affair, as far as I know. I've phoned Helga several times, but she hasn't said, so I can only presume that they never caught the driver.'

Björn sighed. 'A pity, but these things happen. What does Austin think of you staying on?'

Alex had not expected this question, and looked at him in surprise. 'We haven't discussed it.'

He pursed his lips. 'A strange way to carry on. I thought you'd have everything settled by now. Whenever I've seen you two together you've always been deep in conversation.'

It was gratifying to know that he'd noticed. 'Austin's trying to interest me in geology,' she explained.

He took her hand again. 'This is goodbye, then. Thank you for helping me out, and I'm sorry about the mix-up in the first place.'

She tried to speak, but a sudden breathlessness tightened her throat. Her eyes searched his face as if trying to impress every feature into her memory— not that she needed to; it was already there and would be for the rest of her life.

Smiling briefly, Alex snatched away her hand, and missed the slight frown her action caused as she bent to flick an imaginary speck of dust from the knee of her trousers. 'I'm sorry too,' she mumbled. 'I did try—you must believe me.'

'Of course I do,' he agreed quietly.

But Alex felt as though he were humouring her, and turned away before he saw the hurt in her eyes.

'Goodbye, Björn,' she whispered, and hurried over to Austin.

'So he didn't offer to keep you on,' he said after one look at her face. 'I can't say I'm sorry, but I can guess how you feel and you have my sympathy.'

She squeezed his arm. 'I don't know what I'd do without you,' and on a sudden impulse, 'do you have to return to England?'

'Well—I do have some holiday left.'

'Then come and stay with Helga and Jón. I'm sure they'll be pleased to put you up, especially as you're a friend of mine.'

He thought for a minute. 'It would be even better if you could say I was your fiancé. How about it, Alex? I was going to wait until we got back to England before I asked you to marry me, but why should I? Let's get engaged now.'

Alex had never seen him so excited. She had known the question would come and that her answer would be yes; he would make a solid dependable husband and he obviously adored her, so she laughed, 'Why not?' But he did not know that her gaiety was forced, her laugh brittle, and that she was fighting a tremendous battle to keep back the tears.

When she looked round Björn had gone. So that was the end! He did not really care what happened to her now. It took an effort to appear bright and cheerful after that, but she did not want to spoil Austin's happiness. He was so good to her. He knew how she felt about Björn, but was still prepared to risk marrying her. She couldn't let him down. Not now.

As Alex had expected, Helga was only too pleased to prepare a room for Austin, and although she looked at Alex a trifle strangely when she introduced him as her fiancé, she asked no questions at that stage.

Alex was pleased to see Jón up and about, but he looked far from well and she guessed the ordeal had taken a lot more out of him than he admitted. He made light of the affair when questioned, but Helga shook her head, warning Alex not to remind him of the incident.

'It makes his head ache to think about it,' she explained later when they were alone in the kitchen. 'I try not to mention it.'

'I'm sorry I had to rush off and leave you,' said Alex, 'I felt so guilty.'

'Don't be silly, there was nothing you could do. I'm surprised Björn never phoned, though. He's usually so considerate.'

Alex blushed. 'That was my fault. I'm afraid I never told him.'

'Why ever not?' asked Helga in surprise.

'He was in a terrible mood when I got back; he didn't even give me chance to explain.'

'Sit down,' said Helga sternly. 'I want to ask you what's going on. Who's this young man you've got yourself engaged to? What about Björn?'

Alex smiled sadly. 'I still love him, Helga, but it's no use. He treated me like a child half the time and an idiot the rest.'

'Now you're exaggerating.'

'It's true,' Alex protested. 'He's been at my throat the whole trip. The things he's blamed on me are nobody's business.'

Helga frowned. 'And where does Austin fit into all this?'

'It's difficult to explain,' grimaced Alex. 'We got on well right from the beginning, but there was nothing in it until Juliet—you remember I told you about her—started trying to make trouble. She thought I was after Björn and wanted him herself. So Austin and I decided to pretend we were better friends than we actually were, just to keep Juliet off my back.'

'And what did Björn think of Juliet?'

'He seemed very fond of her. I'm sure he had no idea how she'd spoken to me.'

'I'd soon have told him,' asserted Helga strongly, 'but go on.'

'There's not much more to tell. I realised eventually that there could never be anything between Björn and me, and as I'm very fond of Austin——'

'You got engaged to him as the next best thing to do?'

'Something like that. He'll make a good husband.'

'But will you make a good wife? Marriage is for ever. What if you fall in love with someone else—or Björn comes to his senses?'

'And pigs will fly,' scoffed Alex. 'Anyway, I'm not married yet, so why are we talking like this?'

'I'll put the kettle on,' laughed Helga. 'A cup of coffee will make us feel better.'

The week passed pleasantly, and Alex felt that Helga and Jón had accepted Austin. Away from Björn's disturbing influence she was able to give him her devoted attention, and he seemed very happy in his new-found relationship.

On Friday Austin said he ought to see about his return ticket. 'How about you?' he added. 'Are you staying or coming back with me? I shall understand if you don't want to come.'

He was nice, thought Alex. She would go a long way to find anyone better.

'I think I will come,' she said at length, 'Jón's nearly better now, and Helga will manage.'

The truth was she wanted to get away from Iceland. It was impossible to forget Björn complently. He haunted her waking and sleeping hours so that she knew she would get no peace until she was out of the country. She loved Iceland, and so too the man whose home the island was, but she must put them both from her mind. This was a period in her life best forgotten.

'I'm glad,' said Austin. 'You'll soon forget Björn once we're home.' It was the first time he had mentioned the other man, yet Alex knew he must have been on his mind. 'I'll take you to visit my parents in Sussex before we go to London. I know Mother will want us to be married in the village church— you won't mind? She never had a daughter, and she's looking forward to the day I get married. She just loves organising.'

Alex let him carry on, scarcely listening. It was easier to have everything arranged.

She was alone when the door opened again. Thinking Austin had returned, she did not move. It was not until he called her name that she looked up.

'Björn!' Unable to hide her joy, she stood up and faced him.

The warmth of his response turned her legs to jelly and she groped for the chair behind her. He stepped forward quickly and put his hands on her shoulders. 'Helga said I'd find you in here. You're looking very radiant. Being in love obviously suits you.'

How true those words were—she could feel the love shining in her eyes and was unable to do anything about it. She didn't stop to wonder why he was here; it was sufficient that he had come.

The smoke-grey eyes pierced her own, held her as if hypnotised. 'I was surprised you were still here. I thought you'd be back in England by now.'

'And I thought you'd be away on your next tour,' retorted Alex.

'I start tomorrow. After that there will be no let-up until the end of the season. That's why I came to see Jón and Helga today.'

She couldn't resist asking, 'You've found yourself another courier?'

His eyes twinkled. 'I have—though he won't be as decorative as you.'

'Is that intended as a compliment?'

'You sound surprised. Don't you think I'm capable of noticing a pretty girl?'

'But of course, what man isn't? It's just that you were different with me.' She found it easier to talk to him now that he was no longer her employer. 'I suspected you didn't like me very much.'

He raised his brows. 'Did I ever say that?'

'Not in so many words,' she admitted.

'But I wasn't very kind to you—is that it?'

'Something like that.'

'Perhaps I was a little hard. You see I'd never envisaged a woman in that sort of job—not in my country——'

'And you were determined I wouldn't succeed?' she cut in pertly.

It was easy to laugh now. Björn was different; he was once again the smiling stranger with whom she had fallen in love. Those eyes which had hypnotised her then were again mesmerising her senses, and suddenly she felt she must escape. This was madness. He was looking at her as though she were his most treasured possession.

It couldn't be! Why was he acting so? Only on one other occasion had she seen this expression on his face—love, desire, passion—perhaps all three. She had thought then that she was mistaken—but this time she knew it was not imagination.

His hands were on her arms now, drawing her gently towards him. She could not resist, she did not want to. This was a moment she had dreamed of. Tomorrow she would wonder why, but now—the moment was upon her and she was as desirous of his kisses as he was of hers.

'Alexandra.' His lips brushed her cheek and a soft moan escaped her. She lifted her face, her eyes closed in anticipation. 'Alexandra,' he murmured, tell me——'

But the sentence was never finished. He released her abruptly as the door burst open. Austin came in, looking from Alex's flushed face to Björn, once again calm and controlled with no sign of the passion Alex had seen only seconds earlier. How could he change so? thought Alex, but she was given no time to ponder.

'I hope I'm not intruding?'

'I was kissing Alexandra goodbye,' Björn said blandly. 'I hope you don't mind.'

'Be my guest,' shrugged Austin. 'I just wanted to tell Alex that I've fixed the tickets for tomorrow. We'll be leaving at nine.'

He had gone again before Alex could speak, but the change in Björn was dramatic. His eyes had darkened noticeably and two furrows creased his brow.

'Why didn't you tell me Austin was staying here? I thought he was in England. I don't like making a fool of myself. When I found you here I thought that—well, no, it doesn't matter—but I wanted to find out—oh, damn you, woman!' and turning swiftly he left the room.

Alex sank weakly on to her chair. She felt bemused. Never before had she seen Björn so—so shaken, so unsure of himself—so annoyed with her. If only Austin had not entered at that precise moment! What had Björn been going to ask her, and why had he behaved in such a peculiar manner? That he had wanted to kiss her at all was an enigma. He had already decided she was the type of woman to give herself freely to any man, so what was he up to this time? It was too much to think he might be attracted to her for herself alone. He had made this abundantly clear so many times—yet that look on his face—she could have sworn ...

Shaking her head impatiently, Alex decided the best thing was to push the whole episode from her mind. Björn had gone now, the roar of his car was unmistakable, and there was little chance of their meeting again. The puzzle would remain unsolved.

'Everything all right?' inquired Austin, coming back into the room a few minutes later. 'I must admit I was surprised to find Björn here. What had he got to say?'

'*You* were surprised!' echoed Alex. 'Try and guess how I felt.'

'I thought he seemed—er—very friendly,' and suddenly concerned, 'he didn't ask you to work for him again?'

Alex forced a laugh. 'Not likely, although he was very charming until you burst in, then he went all peculiar. I wish I could understand him.'

'I think I do,' said Austin slowly. 'He didn't fool me when he said he was kissing you goodbye; he was too intense. Oh, he altered as soon as he saw me me, but not quickly enough. I saw the look on his face. He's in love with you, Alex, whether he knows it or not.'

'That's ridiculous,' she exploded. 'If he loves me and I love him, where's the problem?'

'Because neither of you will admit it. You're as stubborn as mules.' He gave her a long, considering look. 'Perhaps you ought to stay here after all. Who knows what miracle might happen?'

'Oh, no,' said Alex quickly, 'I know Björn better

than you. I *must* get away. He hates me. He's only experimenting when he kisses me.' Her face crumpled. How she wished Austin was right, but he couldn't be. If Björn truly loved her he would admit it. She imagined he was the type of man to always get what he wanted. No—Austin was wrong. She would carry on with her plans as though Björn hadn't been here today. Marriage to Austin was the only answer.

But it didn't work out exactly like that. After only one week back in England Alex began to realise how impossible marriage to Austin would be. He was right when he said his parents would adore her, but she on her part found his mother intolerable. She was very dominant, and overruled any suggestions Alex herself made so far as the wedding was concerned. She even chose a nearby cottage which she offered to buy them as a wedding present.

'Oh no,' exclaimed Alex, when she and Austin were alone, 'I couldn't live there, so near to your mother. Anyway, I want to choose my own home.'

He bristled defensively. 'What's wrong with my mother? I think she's being wonderful, the way she's organising the whole affair.'

'That's the trouble,' said Alex, 'I'm not allowed to do anything, or even voice my opinion.'

'We're not good enough for you, is that what you mean?' he demanded.

'Of course not.' Alex tried to soften her voice. They were arguing already! What would it be like once they were married? She couldn't imagine Mrs

Maddison sitting back and letting Alex run her own life without any interference.

And so the argument went on, until at last Alex declared she had had enough and was returning to her grandfather's house. 'It won't work,' she cried, 'I see that now. I'm sorry, Austin, I should have known.'

He grimaced. 'Perhaps I'm expecting too much. I know you still love Björn and it must seem as though I'm rushing you. How about waiting a while? It will give you chance to get over him, and also get used to my mother. She's only doing what she thinks is best. She knows you're alone, and——'

'I know.' She laid a hand on his arm. 'But I don't really think I shall ever forget Björn. I thought I would, once we'd left Iceland—but it's impossible. No, I'm going back to London. I need to be alone to sort things out in my mind.'

'I'll miss you, Alex,' he said quietly, 'though in my heart of hearts I think I knew this would happen. Björn's a fool. He doesn't know what he's missing.'

And so Alex went back to London. The house in Bayswater was strangely quiet and empty, but she kept herself occupied by sorting out her grandfather's papers and personal possessions—a task she had previously shunned.

She half expected Gerard to call round once he discovered she was back; it was funny she had heard nothing from him since the day she announced her intention of working in Iceland. And then one day she was told by a mutual friend that Gerard was married. It was a shock to find out that the staid and somewhat pompous Gerard had defied all conventions and got married by special licence only days after meeting the girl who was now his wife. It amused Alex tremendously, and she felt no regrets that he had passed so completely out of her life.

It was not a particularly good summer. Austin telephoned regularly, but Alex gave him no encouragement. She could see now that they would never be happy and wondered why she had ever imagined they might. It was no good marrying without love.

Helga wrote occasionally and Alex eagerly opened her letters, hoping that there might be some news of Björn, but for some reason she never mentioned him, and Alex was afraid to ask, for fear of giving away her own feelings.

He was perpetually in her thoughts, no matter how she tried to forget him. She would sometimes indulge in dreams when he turned up at the door declaring that he loved her and could not live without her, or else he would beg her to go back and work for him, which eventually resulted in a declaration of his love.

Through these flights of fantasy she kept alive her memories of Björn—whether it was a good thing she did not know—but for the time being her innermost thoughts were the only comfort she had, and as summer turned into autumn and the greens changed to russet and gold, so too did her dreams take on a rosy hue. She lived in a world of her own—she was a prisoner of love, and knew not how to escape.

When one day in September she opened the door to find Björn standing there, she thought she must still be dreaming. She put out her hand to touch him. 'It really is you! I—I thought I was imagining things.'

He was just as she remembered him, tall and proud; arrogant, yet strangely humble this day. He did not smile, nor did he appear stern. His eyes never left her face and Alex was aware that his physical attraction was as strong as ever. Her hand fluttered to her throat; she felt breathless, exhilarated and at the same time puzzled.

'Well, aren't you going to ask me in?'

'I'm sorry,' she murmured, 'do forgive me. I—I was so surprised.' She stood back and allowed him to enter. 'Would you like a drink? There's still some of my grandfather's whisky.'

'That's very kind of you,' he said, and followed her into the elegantly-furnished room. Nothing but the best had been good enough for her grandfather, and Alex felt pleased that Björn should see her in these gracious surroundings. She only wished that she had had a little warning, so that she could have changed and combed her hair.

She was so intensely aware of him standing beside her as she poured the drinks that her hand trembled as she handed him one of the glasses. Why was he looking at her so strangely, as though seeing her for the first time?

She moved away and switched on the fire, more for something to do than because she was cold. In fact Björn's presence had brought a sudden warmth to her skin and a colour to her cheeks that made her look even more attractive than usual. Her raven hair was loose about her shoulders and her eyes shone with an unusual brilliance. To the man standing opposite she had never appeared more desirable, but she did not know this.

'Please sit down,' she said, lowering herself into an armchair on the opposite side of the hearth. The whisky had helped steady her nerves. 'Tell me what brings you to this part of the world.'

He took a long swallow and looked at her quizzically. 'To tell you I had business in London wouldn't be strictly accurate, but it will suffice for now. But I haven't come here to talk about myself, it's you I'm interested in. I went to see Helga the other day and she told me that you weren't going to marry Austin after all.'

Alex's cheeks flamed. 'I wish she hadn't. It can be of no interest to you.'

One eyebrow lifted in that familiar way. 'Oh no? Perhaps she thought it would help me.'

He looked amused and Alex frowned. 'What do you mean? How could it be of any benefit to you?'

'Don't you know, Alexandra? Don't you know?' He put down his glass and studied her face.

Alex's heart beat at a most alarming rate. If he meant what she thought—but no, her imagination was playing tricks again. He couldn't possibly.

'What are you trying to tell me?' she whispered.

He rose, at the same time holding out his hands. As if in a dream Alex sailed into his arms. As her lips parted beneath his she knew that this time it was the real thing. Björn *did* love her. His lips left her mouth for a space to caress the soft curve of her cheek, the pink tips of her ears, her throat, her neck, returning hungrily for more kisses which Alex returned with an intensity that amazed her. Never before had she risen to such heights. When he stopped she looked wonderingly at him.

'I love you, Alexandra. I've been a fool and I've hurt you, but at last I've come to my senses.'

'How? Why?' The words were scarcely more than a whisper, and she clung to him as if afraid he might even now disappear.

'Many things. It's been a dreadful summer. My courier didn't turn up, so I had to do without one.'

'Why didn't you send for me?' twinkled Alex.

'How could I? You and Austin—I thought you were——'

'So if Helga hadn't told you about us you wouldn't be here now?'

'Oh, I'd have still come, even if only to attend your wedding. There's something else Helga told me—but I'd rather hear you say that yourself.' His eyes glinted wickedly.

'Wait until I see her!' declared Alex hotly, though she wasn't really annoyed, and when Björn kissed her again she had little difficulty in saying the words he wanted to hear. 'I do love you, Björn. I couldn't stand it when you said horrid things to me. I thought you hated me.'

'I've loved you from the very beginning,' he said, 'from the moment I set eyes on you at the airport.'

'Then why did you treat me so harshly?'

He looked guilty. 'A defence mechanism, I guess. You looked too beautiful to be useful as well. I think I was afraid.'

Björn—afraid? This couldn't be so. She had always regarded him as the strong one. Nothing and no one had ever seemed to deter him.

'You look at me like that,' he continued, 'with eyes full of wonder. It happens, you know. Greater men than I have fallen, though I must admit I wasn't ready.'

'And you fought me every inch of the way,' she teased.

'If I'd known how you felt things would have been different,' he said softly.

'And if you'd known how many times I've wanted to tell you! It was sheer hell.'

'It seems I've given you a pretty rough time one way and another,' he smiled, 'but that will be altered now. When will you marry me, Alexandra? I've suddenly become a very impatient man.'

'There's one thing that bothers me,' she said, 'Juliet! You gave the impression of being very fond of her.'

'You're jealous,' he accused, smiling delightedly. 'But I think we can safely forget all about Mrs Devall.'

Alex looked at him incredulously. '*Mrs?*'

He nodded. 'You were right when you said there was something suspicious about her. She was what you might term an advance party; her husband planned setting up in opposition and she was to find out all she could. I thought she was taking an abnormal amount of interest, but my male vanity would only let me think it was myself who was the attraction.'

'I think maybe you were,' laughed Alex, suddenly realising what Juliet had meant when she declared that herself and Björn two of a kind. 'She lost no time in warning me off you.'

'She did *what*?' he demanded.

'It was after I'd hurt my ankle. She accused me of trying to attract your attention with my helpless little-girl tactics. That was only the first of many times.'

'I wsh you'd told me, Alexandra,' he said, looking concerned. 'She was always so nice when we were together. I really did like her.'

'You wouldn't have listened,' she protested. 'That's where Austin came to my aid. We decided to pretend we were lovers to keep her off my back.'

His eyes narrowed. 'It didn't look very much like pretending to me.'

'Maybe on Austin's part it wasn't,' she said wryly. 'He did say he loved me after a while.'

'I see. It explains a lot. But surely you weren't going to marry the man without loving him?'

Alex grimaced. 'I couldn't get what I wanted, so it seemed the only way out. I was very fond of him.'

'And what was it you wanted?' His voice was deep and held a hint of mockery, but his eyes twinkled as he waited for her reply.

'You know very well it was you,' she returned, feeling her heart race furiously beneath his gaze.

'All the time it was me?' he said gruffly.

Alex nodded.

'I think I knew. That time on the boat—at Lake Mývatn—I was afraid to let myself believe you meant it, though I hated the thought that you could be so free with your kisses. How I must have hurt you!' He touched her face tenderly.

'Tell me more about Juliet,' she questioned. 'How's it going to affect you?'

He smiled mysteriously. 'It won't. I've sold out to them.'

'Björn! What are you saying?' Alex could hardly believe her ears.

'I've sold the business—lock, stock and barrel. It will in future be known as Devall Travel.'

'But why? Was it such a bad year? You've hardly given yourself time to get going.'

'I decided it wouldn't be fair on my wife. It would take up too much of my time.'

'B—but you didn't know I would agree to marry you,' she protested.

Again the mysterious smile. 'I was fairly sure, after my little talk with Helga. My only regret now is that I didn't follow my instincts on that first day. I was old-fashioned enough to want a proper period of courtship, and I didn't think business should be combined with pleasure. It was my own fault that I nearly lost you. Can you ever forgive me?'

'I already have,' she smiled. 'From the minute you walked into this room the past was forgotten.'

'It's more than I deserve,' he said humbly, 'but I'll make it up to you. From now on there will be no more cross words. I intend to see that you're completely happy for the rest of your life.'

'With you beside me, my darling, how could I be otherwise?' and their lips met in an eminently satisfying kiss that told her more surely than any words how deeply he loved her.

In that moment Alex felt as though her heart was ready to burst. She had been so sure that she would never see Bjorn again it was difficult to comprehend that he was here now and soon they would be married. Dear Helga, she must thank her for the part she had played—without her help she would still be here alone, destined to spend her life dreaming of her lost love.

'What are you thinking about?' he asked softly.

She smiled. 'How grateful I am to Helga. Just think, if she hadn't told you we would never have——'

He did not allow her to finish. For several minutes afterwards there was silence in the room, save for the ponderous ticking of the grandfather clock and the beating of two hearts as one.

Did you miss any of these exciting Harlequin Omnibus 3-in-1 volumes?

Each volume contains 3 great novels by one author for only $1.95.
See order coupon.

Violet Winspear

Violet Winspear #3
The Cazalet Bride (#1434)
Beloved Castaway (#1472)
The Castle of the Seven Lilacs (#1514)

Anne Mather

Anne Mather
Charlotte's Hurricane (#1487)
Lord of Zaracus (#1574)
The Reluctant Governess (#1600)

Anne Hampson

Anne Hampson #1
Unwary Heart (#1388)
Precious Waif (#1420)
The Autocrat of Melhurst (#1442)

Betty Neels

Betty Neels
Tempestuous April (#1441)
Damsel in Green (#1465)
Tulips for Augusta (#1529)

Essie Summers

Essie Summers #3
Summer in December (#1416)
The Bay of the Nightingales (#1445)
Return to Dragonshill (#1502)

Margaret Way

Margaret Way
King Country (#1470)
Blaze of Silk (#1500)
The Man from Bahl Bahla (#1530)

Available only by mail!

40 magnificent Omnibus volumes to choose from:

Essie Summers #1
Bride in Flight (#933)
Postscript to Yesterday (#1119)
Meet on My Ground (#1326)

Jean S. MacLeod
The Wolf of Heimra (#990)
Summer Island (#1314)
Slave of the Wind (#1339)

Eleanor Farnes
The Red Cliffs (#1335)
The Flight of the Swan (#1280)
Sister of the Housemaster (#975)

Susan Barrie #1
Marry a Stranger (#1034)
Rose in the Bud (#1168)
The Marriage Wheel (#1311)

Violet Winspear #1
Beloved Tyrant (#1032)
Court of the Veils (#1267)
Palace of the Peacocks (#1318)

Isobel Chace
The Saffron Sky (#1250)
A Handful of Silver (#1306)
The Damask Rose (#1334)

Joyce Dingwell #1
Will You Surrender (#1179)
A Taste for Love (#1229)
The Feel of Silk (#1342)

Sara Seale
Queen of Hearts (#1324)
Penny Plain (#1197)
Green Girl (#1045)

Jane Arbor
A Girl Named Smith (#1000)
Kingfisher Tide (#950)
The Cypress Garden (#1336)

Anne Weale
The Sea Waif (#1123)
The Feast of Sara (#1007)
Doctor in Malaya (#914)

Essie Summers #2
His Serene Miss Smith (#1093)
The Master to Tawhai (#910)
A Place Called Paradise (#1156)

Catherine Airlie
Doctor Overboard (#979)
Nobody's Child (#1258)
A Wind Sighing (#1328)

Violet Winspear #2
Bride's Dilemma (#1008)
Tender Is the Tyrant (#1208)
The Dangerous Delight (#1344)

Kathryn Blair
Doctor Westland (#954)
Battle of Love (#1038)
Flowering Wilderness (#1148)

Rosalind Brett
The Girl at White Drift (#1101)
Winds of Enchantment (#1176)
Brittle Bondage (#1319)

Rose Burghley
Man of Destiny (#960)
The Sweet Surrender (#1023)
The Bay of Moonlight (#1245)

Iris Danbury
Rendezvous in Lisbon (#1178)
Doctor at Villa Ronda (#1257)
Hotel Belvedere (#1331)

Amanda Doyle
A Change for Clancy (#1085)
Play the Tune Softly (#1116)
A Mist in Glen Torran (#1308)

Great value in Reading!
Use the handy order form

Elizabeth Hoy
Snare the Wild Heart
(#992)
The Faithless One
(#1104)
Be More than Dreams
(#1286)

Roumelia Lane
House of the Winds
(#1262)
A Summer to Love
(#1280)
Sea of Zanj (#1338)

Margaret Malcolm
The Master of
Normanhurst (#1028)
The Man in Homespun
(#1140)
Meadowsweet (#1164)

Joyce Dingwell #2
The Timber Man (#917)
Project Sweetheart
(#964)
Greenfingers Farm
(#999)

Marjorie Norell
Nurse Madeline of Eden
Grove (#962)
Thank You, Nurse
Conway (#1097)
The Marriage of Doctor
Royle (#1177)

Anne Durham
New Doctor at
Northmoor (#1242)
Nurse Sally's Last
Chance (#1281)
Mann of the Medical
Wing (#1313)

Henrietta Reid
Reluctant Masquerade
(#1380)
Hunter's Moon (#1430)
The Black Delaney
(#1460)

Lucy Gillen
The Silver Fishes
(#1408)
Heir to Glen Ghyll
(#1450)
The Girl at Smuggler's
Rest (#1533)

Anne Hampson #2
When the Bough Breaks
(#1491)
Love Hath an Island
(#1522)
Stars of Spring (#1551)

Essie Summers #4
No Legacy for Lindsay
(#957)
No Orchids by Request
(#982)
Sweet Are the Ways
(#1015)

Mary Burchell #3
The Other Linding Girl
(#1431)
Girl with a Challenge
(#1455)
My Sister Celia (#1474)

Susan Barrie #2
Return to Tremarth
(#1359)
Night of the Singing
Birds (#1428)
Bride in Waiting
(#1526)

Violet Winspear #4
Desert Doctor (#921)
The Viking Stranger
(#1080)
The Tower of the Captive
(#1111)

Essie Summers #5
Heir to Windrush Hill
(#1055)
Rosalind Comes Home
(#1283)
Revolt — and Virginia
(#1348)

Doris E. Smith
To Sing Me Home
(#1427)
Seven of Magpies
(#1454)
Dear Deceiver (#1599)

Katrina Britt
Healer of Hearts
(#1393)
The Fabulous Island
(#1490)
A Spray of Edelweiss
(#1626)

Betty Neels #2
Sister Peters in
Amsterdam (#1361)
Nurse in Holland
(#1385)
Blow Hot — Blow Cold
(#1409)

Amanda Doyle #2
The Girl for Gillgong
(#1351)
The Year at Yattabilla
(#1448)
Kookaburra Dawn
(#1562)

Complete and mail this coupon today!